# BULLY!

*a novella by*

# MIKE RESNICK

**PHOENIX PICK BOOKLETS**

*an imprint of*

Rockville, Maryland

ISBN: 978-1-61242-121-6

**www.PhoenixPick.com**
**Great Science Fiction at Great Prices**

Published by Phoenix Pick
*an imprint of Arc Manor*
P. O. Box 10339
Rockville, MD 20849-0339
www.ArcManor.com

# I.

The date was January 8, 1910.

\* \* \*

*"At midnight we had stopped at the station of Koba, where we were warmly received by the district commissioner, and where we met half a dozen of the professional elephant hunters, who for the most part make their money, at hazard of their lives, by poaching ivory in the Congo. They are a hard-bit set, these elephant poachers; there are few careers more adventurous, or fraught with more peril, or which make heavier demands upon the daring, the endurance, and the physical hardihood of those who follow them. Elephant hunters face death at every turn, from fever, from the assaults of warlike native tribes, from their conflicts with their giant quarry; and the unending strain on their health and strength is tremendous."*—Theodore Roosevelt

## AFRICAN GAME TRAILS

*". . . When we were all assembled in my tent and champagne had been served out to everyone except Roosevelt—who insisted on drinking non-intoxicants, though his son Kermit joined us—he raised his glass and gave the toast 'To the Elephant Poachers of the Lado Enclave.' As we drank with him one or two of us laughingly protested his bluntness, so he gravely amended his toast to 'The Gentleman Adventurers of Central Africa', 'for,' he added, 'that is the title by which you would have been known in Queen Elizabeth's time.'*

*"A real man, with the true outdoor spirit, the ex-President's sympathy with and real envy of the life we were leading grew visibly as the evening advanced; and he finally left us with evident reluctance. I, for one, was shaken by the hand three times as he made for the door on three separate occasions; but each time, after hesitatingly listening to the beginning of some new adventure by one of the boys, he again sat down to hear another page from our every-day life. We even urged him to chuck all his political work and come out like the great white man he was, and join us. If he would do this, we promised to put a force under his command to organize the hunting and pioneering business of Central Africa, and perhaps make history. He was, I believe, deeply moved by this offer; and long afterwards he told a friend that no honor ever paid him had impressed and tempted him like that which he received from the poachers of the Lado Enclave."*—John Boyes

## THE COMPANY OF ADVENTURERS

\* \* \*

Roosevelt walked to the door of the tent, then paused and turned back to face Boyes.

"A force, you say?" he asked thoughtfully, as a lion coughed and a pair of hyenas laughed maniacally in the distance.

"That's right, Mr. President," said Boyes, getting to his feet. "I can promise you at least fifty men like ourselves. They may not be much to look at, but they'll be men who aren't afraid to work or to fight, and each and every one of them will be loyal to you, sir."

"Father, it's getting late," called Kermit from outside the tent.

"You go along," said Roosevelt distractedly. "I'll join you in a few minutes." He turned back to Boyes. "Fifty men?"

"That's right, Mr. President."

"Fifty men to tame the whole of Central Africa?" mused Roosevelt.

Boyes nodded. "That's right. There's seven of us right here; we could have the rest assembled inside of two weeks."

"It's very tempting," admitted Roosevelt, trying to suppress a guilty smile. "It would be a chance to be both a boy and a President again."

"The Congo would make one hell of a private hunting preserve, sir," said Boyes.

The American was silent for a moment, and finally shook his massive head. "It couldn't be done," he said at last. "Not with fifty men."

"No," said Boyes. "I suppose not."

"There are no roads, no telephones, no telegraph lines." Roosevelt paused, staring at the flickering lanterns that illuminated the interior of the tent. "And the railway ends in Uganda."

"No access to the sea, either," agreed Boyes pleasantly, as the lion coughed again and a herd of hippos started bellowing in the nearby river.

"No," said Roosevelt with finality. "It simply couldn't be done—not with fifty men, not with five thousand."

Boyes grinned. "Not a chance in the world."

"A man would have to be mad to consider it," said Roosevelt.

"I suppose so, Mr. President," said Boyes.

Roosevelt nodded his head for emphasis. "Totally, absolutely mad."

"No question about it," said Boyes, still grinning at the burly American. "When do we start?"

"Tomorrow morning," said Roosevelt, his teeth flashing as he finally returned Boyes' grin. "By God, it'll be bully!"

## II.

"Father?"

Roosevelt, sitting on a chair in front of his tent, continued staring through his binoculars.

"Kermit, you're standing in front of a lilac-breasted roller and a pair of crowned cranes."

Kermit didn't move, and finally Roosevelt put his binoculars down on a nearby table. He pulled a notebook out of his pocket and began scribbling furiously.

"Remarkable bird viewing here," he said as he added the roller and the cranes to his list. "That's 34 species I've seen today, and we haven't even had breakfast yet." He looked up at his son. "I love these chilly Ugandan nights and mornings. They remind me of the Yellowstone. I trust you slept well?"

"Yes, I did."

"Wonderful climate," said Roosevelt. "Just wonderful!"

"Father, I'd like to speak to you for a few moments, if I may."

Roosevelt carefully tucked the notebook back into his breast pocket. "Certainly," he replied. "What would you like to talk about?"

Kermit looked around, found another canvas chair, carried it over next to his father, and sat down on it.

"This entire enterprise seems ill-conceived, Father."

Roosevelt seemed amused. "That's your considered opinion, is it?"

"One man can't civilize a country half the size of the United States," continued Kermit. "Not even you."

"Kermit, when I was twelve years old, the best doctors in the world told me I'd always be underweight and sickly," said Roosevelt. "But when I was nineteen, I was the lightweight boxing champion of Harvard."

"I know, Father."

"Don't interrupt. People told me I couldn't write a proper sentence, but I've written twenty books, and four of them have been best-sellers. They told me that politics was no place for a young man, but when I was 24 I was Speaker of the House of the New York State Legislature. They told me that law and order had no place in the West, but I went out and single-handedly captured three armed killers in the Dakota Bad Lands during the Winter of the Blue Snow." Roosevelt paused. "Even my Rough Riders said we couldn't take San Juan Hill; I took it." He stared at his son. "So don't tell me what I can't do, Kermit."

"But this isn't like anything else you've done," persisted Kermit.

"What better reason is there to do it?" said Roosevelt with a delighted grin.

"But—"

"Ex-Presidents are supposed to sit around in their rocking chairs and only come out for parades. Well, I'm 51 years old, and I'm not ready to retire yet. Another opportunity like this may never come along." Roosevelt gazed off to the west, toward the Congo. "Think of it, Kermit! More than half a million square miles, filled with nothing but animals and savages and a few missionaries. The British and French and Portuguese and Belgians and Italians all have had their chance at this continent; Africa ought to have one country developed by someone who will bring them American know-how and American democracy and American values. We're a rustic, frontier race ourselves; who better to civilize yet another frontier?" He paused, envisioning a future that was as clear to him as the present. "And think of the natural resources! We'll turn it into a protectorate, and give it favored nation trading status. There's lumber here to build thirty million houses, and where we've cleared the forests away we'll create farms and cities. It will be America all over again—only this time there will be no slavery, no genocide practiced against an indigenous people, no slaughter of the buffalo. I'll use America not as a blueprint, but as a first draft, and I'll learn from our past mistakes."

"But it *isn't* another America, Father," said Kermit. "It's a harsh, savage country, filled with hundreds of tribes whose only experience with white men is slavery."

"Then they'll be happy to find a white man who is willing to redress the balance, won't they?" replied Roosevelt with a confident smile.

"What about the legalities involved?" persisted Kermit. "The Congo is a Belgian colony."

"They've had their chance, and they've muddled it badly." Roosevelt paused. "Suppose you let *me* worry about the Belgians."

Kermit seemed about to argue the point, then realized the fruitlessness of further debate. "All right," he said with a sigh.

"Was there anything else?"

"Yes," said Kermit. "What do you know about this man Boyes?"

"The man's a true pioneer," said Roosevelt admiringly. "He should have been an American."

Kermit shook his head. "The man's a scalawag."

"That's your conclusion after being wined and dined in his tent for a single evening?"

"No, Father. But while you were taking your morning walk and watching birds, I was talking to some of his companions about him. They thought they were bragging about him, and telling me stories that would impress me—but what I heard gave me a true picture of the man."

"For example?" asked Roosevelt.

"He's always in trouble—with the law, with the British army, with the Colonial Office." Kermit paused. "They've tried to deport him from East Africa twice. Did you know that?"

"Certainly I know it," answered Roosevelt. Suddenly he grinned and pointed to a small book that was on the table next to his binoculars. "I spent most of the night reading his memoirs. Remarkable man!"

"Then you know that the British government arrested him for . . ." Kermit searched for the word.

"Dacoity?"

Kermit nodded. "Yes."

"Do you know what it means?" asked his father.

"No," admitted Kermit.

"In this particular case, it means that he signed a treaty with the Kikuyu and got them to open their land to white settlement, and some higher-up in the Colonial government felt that Mr. Boyes was usurping his authority." Roosevelt chuckled. "So they sent a squad of six men into Kikuyuland to arrest him, and they found him surrounded by five thousand armed warriors. And since none of the arresting officers cared very much for the odds, Mr. Boyes volunteered to march all the way to Mombasa on his own recognizance." Roosevelt paused and grinned. "When he walked into court with his five thousand Kikuyu, the case was immediately thrown out." He laughed. "Now, that's a story that could have come out of our own Wild West."

"There were other stories, too, Father," said Kermit. "Less savory stories."

"Good," said Roosevelt. "Then he and I will have something to talk about on the way to the Congo."

"You know, of course, that he's the so-called White King of the Kikuyu."

"And I'm an honorary Indian chief. We have a lot in common."

"You have nothing in common," protested Kermit. "You *helped* our Indians. Boyes became king through deceit and treachery."

"He walked into a savage kingdom that had never permitted a white man to enter it before, and within two years he became the king of the entire Kikuyu nation. That's just the kind of man I need for the work at hand."

"But Father—"

"This is a harsh, savage land, Kermit, and I'm embarking on an enterprise that is neither for the timid nor the weak," said Roosevelt with finality. "He's the man I want."

"You're certain that you won't reconsider?"

Roosevelt shook his head. "The subject is closed."

Kermit stared at his father for a long moment, then sighed in defeat.

"What shall I tell Mother?"

"Edith will understand," said Roosevelt. "She has always understood. Tell her I'll send for her as soon as I've got a proper place to house us all." Suddenly he grinned again. "Maybe we should send for your sister Alice immediately. If there's any native opposition, she can terrify them into submission, just the way she used to do with my Cabinet."

"I'm being serious, Father."

"So am I, Kermit. America's never had an empire, and doesn't want one—but I made us a world power, and if I can increase our influence on a continent where we've yet to gain a foothold, then it's my duty to do so."

"And it'll be such fun," suggested Kermit knowingly.

Roosevelt flashed his son another grin. "It will be absolutely bully!"

Kermit stared at his father for a moment. "If I can't talk you out of this enterprise, I wish you'd let me stay here with you."

Roosevelt shook his head. "Someone has to make sure all the trophies we've taken get to the American Museum on schedule. Besides, if we both stay here, the press will be sure I died during the safari. You've got to go back and tell them about the work I'm doing here." Suddenly he frowned. "Oh, and you'll have to see my editor at Scribner's and tell him that I'll be a little late on the safari manuscript. I'll start working on it as soon as we set up a permanent camp." He paused again. "Oh, yes. Before you woke up this morning, I gave a number of letters to Mr. Cunninghame, who will accompany you for the remainder of the journey. I want you to mail them when you get back to the States. The sooner we get some engineers and heavy equipment over here, the better."

"Heavy equipment?"

"Certainly. We've got a lot of land to clear and a railway to build." A superb starling walked boldly up to the mess tent, looking for scraps, and Roosevelt instantly withdrew his notebook and began scribbling again.

"The Congo's in the middle of the continent," Kermit pointed out. "It will be very difficult to bring in heavy equipment from the coast."

"Nonsense," scoffed Roosevelt. "The British disassembled their steamships, transported them in pieces, and then reassembled them on Lake Victoria and Lake Nyasa. Are you suggesting that Americans, who could build the Panama Canal and crisscross an entire continent with railroads, can't find a way to transport bulldozers and tractors to the Congo?" He paused. "You just see to it that those letters are delivered. The rest will take care of itself."

Just then Boyes approached them.

"Good morning, Mr. Boyes," said Roosevelt pleasantly. "Are we ready to leave?"

"We can break camp whenever you wish, Mr. President," said Boyes. "But one of our natives tells me there's a bull elephant carrying at least one hundred and thirty pounds a side not five miles from here."

"Really?" said Roosevelt, standing up excitedly. "Is he certain? I never saw ivory that large in Kenya."

"This particular boy's not wrong very often," answered Boyes. "He says this bull is surrounded by three or four *askaris*—young males—and that he's moving southeast. If we were to head off in *that* direction"—he pointed across the river to an expanse of dry, acacia-studded savannah—"we could probably catch up with him in a little less than three miles."

"Have we time?" asked Roosevelt, trying unsuccessfully to hide his eagerness.

Boyes smiled. "The Congo's been waiting for someone to civilize it for millions of years, Mr. President. I don't suppose another day will hurt."

Roosevelt turned to his son and shook his hand. "Have a safe trip, Kermit. If I bag this elephant, I'll have his tusks sent on after you."

"Good-bye, Father."

Roosevelt gave the young man a hug, and then went off to get his rifle.

"Don't worry, son," said Boyes, noting the young man's concern. "We'll take good care of your father. The next time you see him, he'll be the King of the Congo."

"President," Kermit corrected him.

"Whichever," said Boyes with a shrug.

## III.

It took Roosevelt six hours to catch up with his elephant, and the close stalk and kill took another hour. The rest of the day was spent removing the tusks and—at the ex-President's insistence—transporting almost three hundred pounds of elephant meat to the porters who had remained with Kermit.

It was too late to begin the trek to the Congo that day, but their little party was on the march shortly after sunrise the next morning. The savannah slowly changed to woodland, and finally, after six days, they came to the Mountains of the Moon.

"You're a remarkably fit man, Mr. President," remarked Boyes, as they made their first camp in a natural clearing by a small, clear stream at an altitude of about 6,000 feet.

"A healthy mind and a healthy body go hand-in-hand, John," replied Roosevelt. "It doesn't pay to ignore either of them."

"Still," continued Boyes, "once we cross the mountains, I think we'll try to find some blooded horses to ride."

"Blooded?" repeated Roosevelt.

"Horses that have already been bitten by the tsetse fly and survived," answered Boyes. "Once they've recovered from the disease, they're immune to it. Such animals are worth their weight in gold out here."

"Where will we find them, and how much will they cost?"

"Oh, the Belgian soldiers will have some," answered Boyes easily. "And they'll cost us two or three bullets."

"I don't understand."

Boyes grinned. "We'll kill a couple of elephants and trade the ivory for the horses."

"You're a resourceful man, Mr. Boyes," said Roosevelt with an appreciative grin.

"Out here a white man's either resourceful or he's dead," answered Boyes.

"I can well imagine," replied Roosevelt. He stared admiringly at the profusion of birds and monkeys that occupied the canopied forest that surrounded the clearing. "It's beautiful up here," he commented. "Pleasant days, brisk nights, fresh air, clear running water, game all around us. A man could spend his life right here."

"*Some* men could," said Boyes. "Not men like us."

"No," agreed Roosevelt with a sigh. "Not men like us."

"Still," continued Boyes, "there's no reason why we can't spend two or three days here. We'll be meeting our party on the other side of the mountains, but they probably won't arrive for another week to ten days. It will take time for word of our enterprise to circulate through the Lado."

"Good!" said Roosevelt. "It'll give me time to catch up on my writing." He paused. "By the way, where did you plan to pitch my tent?"

"Wherever you'd like it."

"As close to the stream as possible," answered Roosevelt. "It's really quite a lovely sight to wake up to."

"No reason why not," said Boyes. "I haven't seen any crocs or hippos about." He gave a brief command to the natives, and pointed to the spot Roosevelt had indicated.

"Please make sure the American flag is stationed in front of it," said Roosevelt. "Oh, and have my books placed inside it."

"You know," said Boyes, "we're using two boys just to carry your books, Mr. President. Perhaps we could leave some of them behind when we break camp and push inland."

Roosevelt shook his head. "That's out of the question: I'd be quite lost without access to literature. If we're short of manpower, we'll leave my rifle behind and have my gunbearer carry one of the book boxes."

Boyes smiled. "That won't be necessary, Mr. President. It was just a suggestion."

"Good," said Roosevelt with a smile. "Just between you and me, I'd feel almost as lost without my Winchester."

"You handle it very well."

"I'm just a talented amateur," answered Roosevelt. "I'm not in a class with you professional hunters."

Boyes laughed. "I'm no professional."

"You were hunting for ivory when we met."

"I was trying to increase my bank account," answered Boyes. "The ivory was just a means to an end. Karamojo Bell is a real hunter, or your friend Selous. I'm just an entrepreneur."

"Don't be so modest, John," said Roosevelt. "You managed to amass quite a pile of ivory. You couldn't do that if you weren't an expert hunter."

"Would you like to know how I actually went about collecting that ivory?" asked Boyes with a grin.

"Certainly."

"I don't know the first thing about tracking game, so I stopped at a British border post, explained that I was terrified of elephants, and slipped the border guards a few pounds to mark the major concentrations on a map of the Lado Enclave so I could avoid them."

Roosevelt laughed heartily. "Still, once you found the herds, you obviously knew what to do."

Boyes shrugged. "I just went where there was no competition."

"I thought the Enclave was filled with ivory hunters."

"Not in the shoulder-high grass," answered Boyes. "No way to sight your rifle, or to maneuver in case of a charge."

"How did you manage to hunt under such conditions?"

"I stood on my bearer's shoulders." Boyes chuckled at the memory. "The first few times I used a .475, but the recoil was so powerful that it knocked me off my perch each time I fired it, so in the end I wound up using a Lee-Enfield .303."

"You're a man of many talents, John."

A yellow-vented bulbul, bolder than its companions, suddenly landed in the clearing to more closely observe the pitching of the tents.

"Lovely bird, the bulbul," remarked Roosevelt, pulling out his notebook and entering the time and location where he had spotted it. "It has an absolutely beautiful voice, too."

"You're quite a bird-watcher, Mr. President," noted Boyes.

"Ornithology was my first love," answered Roosevelt. "I published my initial monograph on it when I was fourteen." He paused. "For the longest time, I thought my future would be in ornithology and taxidermy, but eventually I found men more interesting than animals." Suddenly he grinned. "Or at least, more in need of leadership."

"Well, we've come to the right place," replied Boyes. "I think the Congo is probably more in need of leadership than most places."

"That's what we're here for," agreed Roosevelt. "In fact, I think the time has come to begin formulating an approach to the problem. So far we've just been speaking in generalizations; we must have some definite plan to present to the men when we're fully assembled." He paused. "Let's take another look at that map."

Boyes withdrew a map from his pocket and unfolded it.

"This will never do," said Roosevelt, trying to study the map as the wind kept whipping through it. "Let's find a table."

Boyes ordered two of the natives to set up a table and a pair of chairs, and a moment later he and Roosevelt were sitting side by side, with the map laid out on the table and held in place by four small rocks.

"Where are we now?" asked Roosevelt.

"Right about here, sir," answered Boyes, pointing to their location. "The mountains are the dividing line between Uganda and the Congo. We'll have to concentrate our initial efforts in the eastern section."

"Why?" asked Roosevelt. "If we move *here*"—he pointed to a more centrally-located spot—"we'll have access to the Congo River."

"Not practical," answered Boyes. "Most of the tribes in the eastern quarter of the country understand Swahili, and that's the only native language most of our men will be able to speak. Once we get inland we'll run into more than two hundred dialects, and if they speak any civilized language at all, it'll be French, not English."

"I see," said Roosevelt. He paused to consider this information, then stared at the map again. "Now, where does the East African Railway terminate?"

"Over here," said Boyes, pointing. "In Kampala, about halfway through Uganda."

"So we'll have to extend the railway or build a road about 300 miles or more to reach a base in the eastern section of the Congo?"

"That's a very ambitious undertaking, Mr. President," said Boyes dubiously.

"Still, it will have to be done. There's no other way to bring in the equipment we'll need." Roosevelt turned to Boyes. "You look doubtful, John."

"It could take years. The East African Railway wasn't called the Lunatic Line without cause."

Roosevelt smiled confidently. "They called it the Lunatic Line because only a lunatic would spend one thousand pounds per mile of track. Well, if there's one thing Americans can build, it's railroads. We'll do it for a tenth of the cost in a fiftieth of the time."

"If you extend it from Kampala, you'll have to run it over the Mountains of the Moon," noted Boyes.

"We ran railroads over the Rocky Mountains almost half a century ago," said Roosevelt, dismissing the subject. "Now, are there any major cities in the eastern sector? Where's Stanleyville?"

"Stanleyville could be on a different planet, for all the commerce it has with the eastern Congo," replied Boyes. "In fact, most of the Belgian settlements are along the Congo River"—he pointed out the river—"which, as you can see, doesn't extend to the eastern section. There are no railways, no rivers, and no roads connecting the eastern sector to the settlements." He paused. "Initially, this may very well work to our advantage, as it could be months before news of anything we may do will reach them."

"Then what *is* in the east?"

Boyes shrugged. "Animals and savages."

"We'll leave the animals alone and elevate the savages," said Roosevelt. "What's the major tribe there?"

"The Mangbetu."

"Do you know anything about them?"

"Just that they're as warlike as the Maasai and the Zulu. They've conquered most of the other tribes." He paused. "And they're supposed to be cannibals."

"We'll have to put a stop to that," said Roosevelt. He flashed Boyes another grin. "We can't have them going around eating registered voters."

"Especially Republicans?" suggested Boyes with a chuckle.

"Especially Republicans," agreed Roosevelt. He paused. "Have they had much commerce with white men?"

"The Belgians leave them pretty much alone," answered Boyes. "They killed the first few civil servants who paid them a visit."

"Then it would be reasonable to assume that they will be unresponsive to our peaceful overtures?"

"I think you could say so, yes."

"Then perhaps we can draw upon your expertise, John," said Roosevelt. "After all, Kikuyuland was also hostile to white men when you first entered it."

"It was a different situation," explained Boyes. "They were warring among themselves, so I simply placed myself and my gun at the disposal of one of the weaker clans and made myself indispensable to them. Once word got out that I had sided with them and turned the tide of battle, they knew they'd be massacred if I left, so they begged me to stay, and one by one we began assimilating the other Kikuyu clans until we had unified the entire nation." He paused. "The Mangbetu are already united, and I very much doubt that they would appreciate any interference from us." He stared thoughtfully at Roosevelt. "And there's something else."

"What?"

"I didn't enter Kikuyuland to bring them the benefits of civilization. The East African Railway needed supplies for 25,000 coolie laborers, and all I wanted to do was find a cheap source of food that I could resell. I was just trying to make a living, not to change the way the Kikuyu lived." He paused. "African natives are a very peculiar lot. You can shoot their elephants, pull gold and diamonds out of their land, even buy their slaves, and they don't seem to give a damn. But once you start interfering with the way they live, you've got a real problem on your hands."

"There's an enormous difference between American democracy and European colonialism," said Roosevelt firmly.

"Let's hope the residents of the Congo agree, sir," said Boyes wryly.

"They will," said Roosevelt. "You know, John, this enterprise was initially your suggestion. If you feel this way, why have you volunteered to help me?"

"I've made and lost three fortunes on this continent," answered Boyes bluntly. "Some gut instinct tells me that there's another one to be made in the Congo. Besides," he added with a smile, "it sounds like a bully adventure."

Roosevelt laughed at Boyes' use of his favorite term. "Well, at least you're being honest, and I can't ask for more than that. Now let's get back to work." He paused, ordering his thoughts. "It seems to me that as long as the Mangbetu control the area, it makes sense to work through them, to use them as our surrogates until we can educate *all* the natives."

"I suppose so," said Boyes. "Still, we can't just walk in there, tell them that we're bringing them the advantages of civilization, and expect a friendly reception."

"Why not?" said Roosevelt confidently. "The direct approach is usually best."

"They're predisposed to dislike and distrust you, Mr. President."

"They're predisposed to dislike and distrust Belgians, John," answered Roosevelt. "They've never met an American before."

"I don't think they're inclined to differentiate between white men," said Boyes.

"You're viewing them as Democrats," said Roosevelt with a smile. "I prefer to think of them as uncommitted voters."

"I think you'd be better advised to think of them as hostile—and hungry."

"John, when I was President, I used to have a saying: Walk softly, but carry a big stick."

"I've heard it," acknowledged Boyes.

"Well, I intend to walk softly among the Mangbetu—but if worst comes to worst, we'll be carrying fifty big sticks with us."

"I wonder if fifty guns will be enough," said Boyes, frowning.

"We're not coming to slaughter them, John—merely to impress them."

"We might impress them more if we waited for some of your engineers and Rough Riders to show up."

"Time is a precious commodity," answered Roosevelt. "I have never believed in wasting it." He paused. "Bill Taft will almost certainly run for re-election in 1912. I'd like to make him a gift of the Congo as an American protectorate before he leaves office."

"You expect to civilize this whole country in six years?" asked Boyes in amused disbelief.

"Why not?" answered Roosevelt seriously. "God made the whole world in just six days, didn't He?"

## IV.

They remained in camp for two days, with Roosevelt becoming more and more restless to begin his vast undertaking. Finally he convinced Boyes to trek across the mountain range, and a week later they set up a base camp on the eastern border of the Belgian Congo.

The ex-President was overflowing with energy. When Boyes would awaken at sunrise, Roosevelt had already written ten or twelve pages, and was undergoing his daily regimen of vigorous exercise. By nine in the morning he was too restless to remain in camp, and he would take a tracker and a bearer out to hunt some game for the pot. In the heat of the day, while Boyes and the porters slept in the shade, Roosevelt sat in a canvas chair beside his tent, reading from the 60-volume library that accompanied him everywhere. By late afternoon it was time for a long walk and an hour of serious bird-watching, followed by still more writing and then dinner. And always, as he sat beside the fire with Boyes and those poachers who had begun making their way to the base camp, he would speak for hours, firing them with his vision for the Congo and discussing how best to accomplish it. Then, somewhere between nine and ten at night, everyone would go off to bed, and while the others slept, Roosevelt's tent was always aglow with lantern light as he read for another hour.

Boyes decided that if Roosevelt weren't given something substantial to do he might spontaneously combust with nervous energy. Therefore, since 33 members of his little company had already arrived, he broke camp and assumed that the remaining 15 to 20 men would be able to follow their trail.

They spent two days tracking down a large bull elephant and his young *askaris*, came away with fourteen tusks, six of them quite large, and then marched them 20 miles north to a Belgian outpost. They traded the tusks for seven blooded horses, left three of their party behind to acquire more ivory and trade it for the necessary number of horses, and then headed south into Mangbetu country.

They were quite a group. There was Deaf Banks, who had lost his hearing from proximity to repeated elephant gun explosions, but had refused to quit Africa or even leave the bush, and had shot more than 500 elephants. There was Bill Buckley, a burly Englishman who had given up his gold mine in Rhodesia for the white gold he found further north. There was Mickey Norton, who had spent a grand total of three days in cities during the past twenty years. There was Charlie Ross, who had left his native

Australia to become a Canadian Mountie, then decided that the life was too tame and emigrated to Africa. There was Billy Pickering, who had already served two sentences in Belgian jails for ivory poaching, and had his own notions concerning how to civilize the Congo. There were William and Richard Brittlebanks, brothers who had found hunting in the Klondike to be too cold for their taste, and had been poaching ivory in the Sudan for the better part of a decade. There was even an American, Yank Rogers, one of Roosevelt's former Rough Riders, who had no use for the British or the Belgians, but joined up the moment he heard that his beloved Teddy was looking for volunteers. Only the fabled Karamojo Bell, who had just killed his 962nd elephant and was eager to finally bag his thousandth, refused to leave the Lado.

It was understood from the start that Boyes was Roosevelt's lieutenant, and the few who choose to argue the point soon found out just how much strength and determination lay hidden within his scrawny, five-foot-two-inch body. After a pair of fist fights and a threatened pistol duel, which Roosevelt himself had to break up, the chain of command was never again challenged.

They began marching south and west, moving further from the border and into more heavily-forested territory as they sought out the Mangbetu. By the time a week had passed, eighteen more men had joined them.

On the eighth day they came to a large village. The huts were made of dried cattle dung, with thatched roofs, and were clustered around a large central compound.

The inhabitants still spoke Swahili, and explained that the Mangbetu territory was another two days' march to the south. Boyes had the Brittlebanks brothers shoot a couple of bushbuck and a duiker, and made a gift of the meat to the village. He promised to bring them still more meat upon their return, explaining to Roosevelt that this was a standard practice, as one never knew when one might need a friendly village while beating a hasty retreat.

Roosevelt was eager to meet the Mangbetu, and he got his wish two mornings later, shortly after sunrise, when they came upon a Mangbetu village in a large clearing by a river.

"I wonder how many white men they've seen before?" said Roosevelt as a couple of hundred painted Mangbetu, some of them wearing blankets and leopardskin cloaks in the cold morning air, gathered in the center of the village, brandishing their spears and staring at the approaching party.

"They've probably eaten their fair share of Belgians," replied Boyes. "At any rate, they'll know what a rifle is, so we'd better display them."

"They can see that we have them," answered Roosevelt. "That's enough."

"But sir—"

"We've come to befriend them, not decimate them, John. Keep the men back here so they don't feel that we're threatening them," ordered Roosevelt.

"Mr. President, sir," protested Mickey Norton, "please listen to me. I've had experience dealing with savages. We all have. You've got to show 'em who's boss."

"They're not savages, Mr. Norton," said Roosevelt.

"Then what *are* they?"

Roosevelt grinned. "Voters." He climbed down off his horse. "They're our constituents, and I think I'd like to meet them on equal footing."

"Then you'd better take off all your clothes and get a spear."

"That will be enough, Mr. Norton," said Roosevelt firmly.

One old man, wearing a headdress made of a lion's mane and ostrich feathers, seated himself on a stool outside the largest hut, and a number of warriors immediately positioned themselves in front of him.

"Would that be the chief?" asked Roosevelt.

"Probably," said Boyes. "Once in a while, you get a real smart chief who puts some-one else on the throne and disguises himself as a warrior, just in case you're here to kill him. But since the Mangbetu rule this territory, I think we can assume that he's really the headman."

"Nice headdress," commented Roosevelt admiringly. He handed his rifle to Norton. "John, leave your gun behind and come with me. The rest of you men, wait here."

"Would you like us to fan out around the village, sir?" suggested Charlie Ross.

Roosevelt shook his head. "If they've seen rifles before, it won't be necessary, and if they haven't, then it wouldn't do any good."

"Is there anything we *can* do, sir?"

"Try smiling," answered Roosevelt. "Come on, John."

They began approaching the cluster of warriors. A dog raced up, barking furiously. Roosevelt ignored it, and when it saw that it had failed to intimidate them, it lay down in the dust with an almost human expression of disappointment on its face and watched the two men walk past.

The warriors began murmuring, softly at first, then louder, and someone began beating a primal rhythm on the drum.

"The Lado is looking better and better with every step we take," commented Boyes under his breath.

"They're just people, John," Roosevelt assured him.

"With very unusual dietary habits," muttered Boyes.

"If you're worried, I can always have Yank act as my interpreter."

"I'm not worried about dying," answered Boyes. "I just don't want to go down in the history books as the man who led Teddy Roosevelt into a Mangbetu cooking pot."

Roosevelt chuckled. "If it happens, there won't be any survivors to write about it. Now try to be a little more optimistic." He looked ahead at the assembled Mangbetu. "What do you suppose would happen if we walked right up to the chief?"

"He's got a couple of pretty mean-looking young bucks standing on each side of him," noted Boyes. "I wish we had our rifles."

"We won't need them, John," Roosevelt assured him. "I was always surrounded by the Secret Service when I was President—but they never interfered with my conduct of my office."

They were close enough now to smell the various oils that the Mangbetu had rubbed onto their bodies, and to see some of the patterns that had been tattooed onto their faces and torsos.

"Just keep smiling," answered Roosevelt. "We're unarmed, and our men are keeping their distance."

"Why do we have to smile?" asked Boyes.

"First, to show that we're happy to see them," said Roosevelt. "And second, to show them that we don't file our teeth."

The Mangbetu brandished their spears threateningly as Roosevelt reached them, but the old headman uttered a single command and they parted, allowing the two men a narrow path to the chief. When they got to within eight feet of him, however, four large bodyguards stepped forward and barred their way.

"John, tell him that I'm the King of America, and that I bring him greetings and felicitations."

Boyes translated Roosevelt's message. The chief stared impassively at him, and the four warriors did not relax their posture.

"Tell him that my country has no love for the Belgians."

Boyes uttered something in Swahili, and suddenly the old man seemed to show some interest. He nodded his head and responded.

"He says he's got no use for them either."

Roosevelt's smile broadened. "Tell him we're going to be great friends."

Boyes spoke to the chief again. "He wants to know why."

"Because I am going to bring him all the gifts of civilization, and I ask nothing in return except his friendship."

Another brief exchange followed. "He wants to know where the gifts of civilization are."

"Tell him they're too big for our small party of men to carry, but they're on their way."

The chief listened, finally flashed Roosevelt a smile, and turned to Boyes.

"He says any enemy of the Belgians is a friend of his."

Roosevelt stepped forward and extended his hand. The chief stared at it for a moment, then hesitantly held out his own. Roosevelt took it and shook it vigorously. Two of the old man's bodyguards tensed and raised their spears again, but the chief said something to them and they immediately backed off.

"I think you startled them," offered Boyes.

"A good politician always likes to press the flesh, as we say back home," responded Roosevelt. "Tell him that we're going to bring democracy to the Congo."

"There's no word for democracy in Swahili."

"What's the closest approximation?"

"There isn't one."

The chief suddenly began speaking. Boyes listened for a moment, then turned to Roosevelt.

"He suggests that our men leave their weapons behind and come join him in a feast celebrating our friendship."

"What do you think?"

"Maybe he's as friendly as he seems, but I don't think it would be a good idea just yet."

"All right," responded Roosevelt, holding his hand up to his glasses as a breeze brought a cloud of dust with it. "Thank him, tell him that the men have already eaten, but that you and I will accept his gracious invitation while our men guard the village against the approach of any Belgians."

"He says there aren't any Belgians in the area."

"Tell him we didn't see any either, but one can't be too careful in these dangerous times, and that now that we are friends, our men are prepared to die defending his village from his Belgian oppressors."

The chief seemed somewhat mollified, and nodded his acquiescence.

"Did you ever drink *pombe*?" asked Boyes, as the chief arose and invited them into his hut.

"No," said Roosevelt. "What is it?"

"A native beer."

"You know I don't imbibe stimulants, John."

"Well, Mr. President, you're going to have to learn how to imbibe very fast, or you're going to offend our host."

"Nonsense, John," said Roosevelt. "This is a democracy. Every man is free to drink what he wants."

"Since when did it become a democracy?" asked Boyes wryly.

"Since you and I were invited to partake in dinner, rather than constitute it," said Roosevelt. "Now let's go explain all the wonders we're going to bring to the Congo."

"Has it occurred to you that you ought to be speaking to the *people* about democracy, rather than to the hereditary chief?" suggested Boyes wryly.

"You've never seen me charm the opposition, John," said Roosevelt with a confident smile. He walked to the door of the hut, then lowered his head and entered the darkened interior. "Give me three hours with him and he'll be our biggest supporter."

He was wrong. It only took 90 minutes.

## V.

They spent the next two weeks marching deeper into Mangbetu territory. News of their arrival always preceded them, transmitted by huge, eight-foot-drums, and their reception was always cordial, so much so that after the first four villages Roosevelt allowed all of his men to enter the villages.

By their eighth day in Mangbetu country the remainder of their party had caught up with them, bringing enough horses so that all 53 men were mounted. Boyes assigned rotating shifts to construct camps, cook, and hunt for meat, and Roosevelt spent every spare minute trying to master Swahili. He forbade anyone to speak to him in English, and within two weeks he was able to make himself understood to the Mangbetu, although it was another month before he could discuss his visions of a democratic Congo without the aid of a translator.

"A wonderful people!" he exclaimed one night as he, Boyes, Charlie Ross and Billy Pickering sat by one of the campfires, after having enlisted yet another two thousand Mangbetu to their cause. "Clean, bright, willing to listen to new ideas. I have high hopes for our crusade, John."

Boyes threw a stone at a pair of hyenas that had been attracted by the smell of the impala they had eaten for dinner, and they raced off into the darkness, yelping and giggling.

"I don't know," he replied. "Everything's gone smoothly so far, but . . ."

"But what?"

"These people don't have the slightest idea what you're talking about, Mr. President," said Boyes bluntly.

"I was going to mention that myself," put in Charlie Ross.

"Certainly they do," said Roosevelt. "I spent the entire afternoon with Matapoli—that was his name, wasn't it?—and his elders, explaining how we were going to bring democracy to the Congo. Didn't you see how enthused they all were?"

"There's still no word for *democracy* in Swahili," answered Boyes. "They probably think it's something to eat."

"You underestimate them, John."

"I've lived among blacks all my adult life," replied Boyes. "If anything, I tend to over-estimate them."

Roosevelt shook his head. "The problem is cultural, not racial. In America, we have many Negroes who have become doctors, lawyers, scientists, even politicians. There is nothing a white man can do that a Negro can't do, given the proper training and opportunity."

"Maybe American blacks," said Billy Pickering. "But not Africans."

Roosevelt chuckled in amusement. "Just where do you think America's Negroes came from, Mr. Pickering?"

"Not from the Congo, that's for sure," said Pickering adamantly. "Maybe West African blacks are different."

"All men are pretty much the same, if they are given the same opportunities," said Roosevelt.

"I disagree," said Boyes. "I became the King of the Kikuyu, and you're probably going to become President of the Congo. You don't see any blacks becoming king or president of white countries, do you?"

"Give them time, John, and they will."

"I'll believe it when I see it."

"You may not live to see it, and I may not," said Roosevelt. "But one of these days it's going to happen. Take my word for it."

A lion coughed about a hundred yards away. Both men ignored it.

"Well, you're a very learned man, so if you say it's going to happen, then I suppose it is," said Boyes. "But I hope you're also right that I'll be dead and buried when that happy day occurs."

"You know," mused Roosevelt, "maybe I ought to urge some of our American Negroes to come over here. They could become the first generation of congressmen, so to speak."

"A bunch of your freed slaves set up shop in Liberia a few years back," noted Charlie Ross. "The first thing they did was to start rounding up all the native Liberians and sell them into slavery." He snorted contemptuously. "Some democracy."

"This will be different, Mr. Ross," responded Roosevelt. "These will be educated American politicians, who also just happen to be Negroes."

"Their heads would be decorating every village from here to the Sudan a week later," said Pickering with absolute certainty.

"The Belgians may be oppressing the natives now," added Boyes, "but as soon as they leave, it'll be back to tribal warfare as usual." He paused. "Your democracy is going to have exactly as many political parties as there are tribes, no more and no less, and no tribal member will ever vote for anyone other than a tribal brother."

"Nonsense!" scoffed Roosevelt. "If that philosophy held true, I'd never have won a single vote outside of my home state of New York."

"We're not in America, Mr. President," responded Boyes.

"I obviously have more faith in these people than you do, John."

"Maybe that's because I know them better."

Suddenly Roosevelt grinned. "Well, it wouldn't be any fun if it was too easy, would it?"

Boyes smiled wryly. "I think you're in for a little more fun than you bargained for."

"God put us here to meet challenges."

"Oh," said Charlie Ross. "I was *wondering* why He put us here."

"That's blasphemy, Mr. Ross," said Roosevelt sternly. "I won't hear any more of it."

The men fell silent, and a few moments later, when the fire started dying down, Roosevelt went off to his tent to read.

"He's biting off more than he can chew, John," said Billy Pickering when the ex-President was out of earshot.

"Maybe," said Boyes noncommittally.

"There's no maybe about it," said Pickering. "He hasn't lived with Africans. *We* have. You know what they're like."

"There's another problem, too, John," added Ross.

"Oh?" said Boyes.

"I have a feeling he thinks of us as the Rough Riders, all in for the long haul. But the long rains are coming in a couple of months, and I've got to get my ivory to Mombasa before then. So do a lot of the others."

"You're making a big mistake, Charlie," said Boyes. "He's offering us a whole country. There's not just ivory here; there's gold and silver and copper as well, and *somebody* is going to have to administer it. If you leave now, we may not let you come back."

"You'd stop me?" asked Ross, amused.

"I've got no use for deserters," answered Boyes seriously.

"I never signed any enlistment papers. How can I be a deserter?"

"You can be a deserter by leaving the President when he needs every man he can get."

"Look, John," said Ross. "If I thought there was one chance in a hundred that he could pull this off, I'd stay, no question about it. But we've all managed to accumulate some ivory, and we've had a fine time together, and we haven't had to fight the Belgians yet. Maybe it's time to think about pulling out, while we're still ahead of the game."

Boyes shook his head. "He's a great man, Charlie, and he's capable of great things."

"Even if he does what he says he's going to do, do you really want to live in the Congo forever?"

"I'll live anywhere the pickings are easy," answered Boyes. "And if you're smart, so will you."

"I'll have to think about it, John," said Ross, getting up and heading off toward his tent.

"How about you, Billy?" asked Boyes.

"I came here for just one reason," answered Pickering. "To kill Belgians. We haven't seen any yet, so I guess I'll stick around a little longer." Then he, too, got up and walked away.

The little Yorkshireman remained by the dying embers for a few more minutes, wondering how just much time Roosevelt had before everything fell apart.

## VI.

Two months into what Roosevelt termed their "bully undertaking" they finally ran into some organized resistance. To nobody's great surprise, it came not from the various tribes they had been enlisting in their project, but from the Belgian colonial government.

Despite the imminent arrival of the long rains, Roosevelt's entire party was still in the Congo, due mostly to the threats, pleadings, and promise of riches that Boyes had made when the ex- President was out of earshot.

They had made their way through a dense forest and were now camped by a winding, crocodile-infested river. A dozen of the men were out hunting for ivory, and Pickering was scouting about thirty miles to the west with a Mangbetu guide, seeking a location for their next campsite. Three more members of the party were visiting large Mangbetu villages, scheduling visits from the "King of America" and arranging for word to be passed to the leaders of the smaller villages, most of whom wanted to come and listen to him speak of the wonders he planned to bring to the Congo.

Roosevelt was sitting on a canvas chair in front of his tent, his binoculars hung around his neck and a sheaf of papers laid out on a table before him, editing what he had written that morning, when Yank Rogers, clad in his trademark stovepipe chaps and cowboy Stetson, approached him.

"We got company, Teddy," he announced in his gentle Texas drawl.

"Oh?"

Rogers nodded. "Belgians—and they look like they're ready to declare war before lunch."

"Mr. Pickering will be heartbroken when he finds out," remarked Roosevelt wryly. He wiped some sweat from his face with a handkerchief. "Send them away, and tell them we'll only speak to the man in charge."

"In charge of what?" asked Rogers, puzzled.

"The Congo," answered Roosevelt. "We're going to have to meet him sooner or later. Why should we march all the way to Stanleyville?"

"What if they insist?"

"How big is their party?" asked Roosevelt.

"One guy in a suit, six in uniforms," said Rogers.

"Take twenty of our men with you, and make sure they're all carrying their rifles. The Belgians won't insist."

"Right, Teddy."

"Oh, and Yank?"

The American stopped. "Yes?"

"Tell Mr. Boyes not to remove their wallets before they leave."

Rogers grinned. "That little bastard could find an angle on a baseball. You know he's taking ten percent off the top on all the ivory our men shoot?"

"No, I didn't know. Has anyone objected?"

"Not since he went up against Big Bill Buckley and gave him a whipping," laughed Rogers. "I think he's got notions of taking a percentage of every tusk that's shipped out of the Congo from now til Doomsday." He paused. "Well, I'd better round up a posse and go have a powwow with our visitors."

"Do that," said Roosevelt, spotting an insect that was crawling across his papers and flicking it to the ground. "And send Mr. Boyes over here. I think I'd better have a talk with him."

"If you're going to fight him, I think I can get three-to-one on you," said Rogers. "The rest of 'em never saw you take out that machine gun nest single-handed at San Juan Hill; *I* did. Want me to put a little something down for you, Teddy?"

Roosevelt chuckled at the thought. "Maybe a pound or two, if it comes to that. Which," he added seriously, "it won't."

Rogers went off to gather some of the men, and a few minutes later Boyes approached Roosevelt's tent.

"You wanted to see me, Mr. President?" he asked.

"Yes, I did, John."

"Is it anything to do with the Belgians? Yank Rogers said you were sending them away."

"They'll be back," said Roosevelt, wiping his face once again and wondering if he'd ever experienced this much humidity anywhere in America. "Pull up a chair, John."

Boyes did so, and sat down opposite Roosevelt.

"John, Yank tells me that you've got a healthy little business going on here."

"You mean the ivory?" asked Boyes, making no attempt to conceal it.

Roosevelt nodded. "We're not here to get rich, John. We're here to turn the Congo into a democracy."

"There's no law against doing both," said Boyes.

"I strongly disapprove of it, John. It's profiteering."

"I'm not making a single shilling off the natives, Mr. President," protested Boyes. "How can that be profiteering?"

"You're making it off our own people," said Roosevelt. "That's just as bad."

"I was afraid you were going to look at it like that," said Boyes with a sigh. "Look, Mr. President, we're all for civilizing the Congo—but we're grown men, and we've got to make a living. Now, for most of them, that means ivory hunting when we're not busy befriending the natives. Believe me when I tell you that if you were to forbid it, eighty percent of the men would leave."

"I believe you, John," said Roosevelt. "And I haven't stopped them from hunting ivory whenever they've had the time."

"Well, I haven't got any spare time, between running the camp and acting as your second-in-command," continued Boyes, "so if I'm to make any money, it can't be by spending long days in the bush, hunting for ivory. So unless you see fit to pay me a salary, this seems like the most reasonable way of earning some money. It doesn't cost you anything, it doesn't cost the natives anything, and every one of our men knew the conditions before they signed on."

Roosevelt considered Boyes' argument for a moment, then nodded his consent.

"All right, John. Far be it from me to stand in the way of an entrepreneur." He paused for a moment. "But I want you to promise me one thing."

"What?"

"You'll let me know before you indulge in any other plans to get rich."

"Oh, I'm never without plans, Mr. President," Boyes assured him.

"Would you care to confide in me, then?"

"Why not?" replied Boyes with a shrug. "I've got nothing to hide." He leaned forward in his chair. "Once you start putting your railroad through here, you're going to need about ten thousand laborers. Now, I don't know if you're going to draft some workers from the local tribes, or hire a bunch of coolies from British East, or import all your labor from America—but I *do* know that ten thousand men eat a lot of food. I thought I'd set up a little trading company to deal with some of the tribes; you know, give them things they want in exchange for bags of flour and other edibles." He paused. "It'll be the same thing I did with the Kikuyu when they built the Lunatic Line, and I kept 25,000 coolies fed for the better part of two years."

"I don't want you fleecing the same people we're trying to befriend," said Roosevelt. "We're here to liberate this country, not plunder it."

"If they don't like what I have to trade, they don't have to part with their goods," said Boyes. "And if they *do* like it, I'll undersell any competitor by fifty percent, which will save your fledgling treasury a lot of money."

Roosevelt stared at him for a long moment.

"Well?" said Boyes at last.

"John, if you can save us that much money without cheating the natives, get as rich as you like."

Boyes smiled. "I don't mind if I do, Mr. President."

"You're a remarkable man, John."

Boyes shook his head. "I'm just a skinny little guy who had to learn to use his head to survive with all these brawny white hunters."

"I understand you gave one of them quite a lesson in fisticuffs," remarked Roosevelt.

"You mean Buckley? I had no choice in the matter," answered Boyes. "If I'd let him get away with it, by next week they'd all be backing out on their bargain." Suddenly he smiled again. "I gave him a bottle of gin and helped him finish it, and by the next morning we were good friends again."

"You're in the wrong profession, John," said Roosevelt. "You should have been a politician."

"Not enough money in it," answered Boyes bluntly. "But while we're on the subject of politics, why did we run the Belgians off? Sooner or later we're going to have to deal with them."

"It's simply a matter of practicality," answered Roosevelt. "I think we gave them enough of an insult that the governor of the Congo will have to come here in person to prove that we can't get away with such behavior—and the sooner we meet with him, the sooner we can present our demands."

"What, exactly, do we plan to demand?"

"We're going to demand their complete withdrawal from the Congo, and we're going to stipulate that they must make a public statement in the world press that they no longer have any colonial ambitions in Africa."

"You're not asking for much, are you?" said Boyes sardonically.

"The Belgians have no use for it, and it costs them a fortune to administer it." Roosevelt paused. "King Albert can go find another hunting reserve. We've got a nation to build here."

Boyes laughed in amusement. "And you think they're going to turn it over to a force of 53 men?"

"Certainly not," said Roosevelt. "They're going to turn it over to the natives who live here."

Boyes stared intently at Roosevelt. "You're serious, aren't you?"

"That *is* what we've come here for, isn't it?"

"Yes, but—"

"We have a job to do, John, and time is the one irreplaceable commodity in this world. We can't afford to waste it."

"Are you sure you're not being a little premature about this, Mr. President?" asked Boyes. "I thought we'd spend a year building a native army, and—"

"We can't win a war with the Belgians, John."

"Then what kind of pressure can you bring to bear on them?" asked Boyes, puzzled.

"We can threaten to *lose* a war with them."

Boyes frowned. "I don't think I quite understand, sir."

"You will, John," said Roosevelt confidently. "You will."

## VII.

It took the Assistant Governor of the Congo exactly seven weeks to hear of Roosevelt's summary dismissal of his district representative and to trek from Stanleyville to the American's base camp, by which time the rains had come and gone and the ex-President had enlisted not only the entire Mangbetu nation to his cause, but seven lesser tribes as well.

Word of the Belgians' impending arrival reached camp a full week before they actually showed up—"God, I love those drums!" was Roosevelt's only comment—and Yank Rogers and the Brittlebanks brothers were sent out to greet the party and escort them back to camp.

Roosevelt ordered Boyes to send five of their men out on a two-week hunting expedition. When the little Yorkshireman asked what they were supposed to be hunting for, Roosevelt replied that he didn't much care, as long as they were totally out of communication for at least fourteen days. Boyes shrugged, scratched his head, and finally selected five of his companions at random and suggested they do a little ivory hunting far to the south for the two weeks. Since they had virtually shot out the immediate area, he received no objections.

When the Belgian party finally reached the camp, Roosevelt was waiting for them. He had had his men construct a huge table, some thirty feet long and five feet wide, and the moment they dismounted he invited them to join him and his men for lunch. The Assistant Governor, a tall, lean, ambitious man named Gerard Silva, seemed somewhat taken aback by the American's hospitality, but allowed himself and his twenty armed soldiers to be escorted to the table, where a truly magnificent feast of warthog, bushbuck, and guinea fowl awaited them.

Roosevelt's men, such as could fit on one side of the table, sat facing the west, and the Belgian soldiers were seated opposite them. The American sat at the head of the table, and Silva sat at the foot of it, thirty feet away. Under such an arrangement, private discussions between the two leaders was impossible, and Roosevelt encouraged his men to discuss their hunting and exploring adventures, though not more than half a dozen of the Belgian soldiers could speak or understand English.

Finally, after almost two hours, the meal was concluded, and Roosevelt's men—except for Boyes—left the table one by one. Silva nodded to a young lieutenant, and the Belgian soldiers followed suit, clustering awkwardly around their horses. Then Silva stood up, walked down to Roosevelt's end of the table, and seated himself next to the American.

"I hope you enjoyed your meal, Mr. Silva," said Roosevelt, sipping a cup of tea.

"It was quite excellent, Mr . . . ?" Silva paused. "What would you prefer that I call you?"

"Colonel Roosevelt, Mr. Roosevelt, or Mr. President, as you prefer," said Roosevelt expansively.

"It was an excellent meal, Mr. Roosevelt," said Silva in precise, heavily-accented English. He withdrew a cigar and offered one to Roosevelt, who refused it. "A wise decision," he said. "The tobacco we grow here is decidedly inferior."

"You must be anxious to return to Belgium, then," suggested Roosevelt.

"As you must be anxious to return to America," responded Silva.

"Actually, I like it here," said Roosevelt. "But then, I don't smoke."

"A nasty habit," admitted Silva. "But then, so is trespassing."

"*Am* I trespassing?" asked Roosevelt innocently.

"Do not be coy with me, Mr. Roosevelt," said Silva. "It is most unbecoming. You have brought a force of men into Belgian territory for reasons that have not been made clear to us. You have no hunting permit, no visa, no permission to be here at all."

"Are you telling us to leave?"

"I am simply trying to discover your purpose here," said Silva. "If you have come solely for sport, I will personally present you with papers that will allow you to go anywhere you wish within the Congo. If you have come for some other reason, I demand to know what it is."

"I would rather discuss that with the governor himself," responded Roosevelt.

"He is quite ill with malaria, and may not be able to leave Stanleyville for another month."

Roosevelt considered the statement for a moment, then shook his head. "No, we've wasted enough time already. I suppose you'll simply have to take my message to him." He paused. "I suppose it doesn't make much difference. The only thing he'll do is transmit my message to King Albert."

"And what is the gist of your message, Mr. Roosevelt?" asked Silva, leaning forward intently.

"My men and I don't consider ourselves to be in Belgian territory."

Silva smiled humorlessly. "Perhaps you would like me to pinpoint your position on a map. You are indeed within the legal boundaries of the Belgian Congo."

"We know where we are, and we fully agree that we are inside the border of the Congo," answered Roosevelt. "But we don't recognize your authority here."

"Here? You mean right where we are sitting?"

"I mean anywhere in the Congo."

"The Congo is Belgian territory, Mr. Roosevelt."

Roosevelt shook his head. "The Congo belongs to its inhabitants. It's time they began determining their own future."

"That is the most ridiculous thing I have ever heard," said Silva. "It has been acknowledged by all the great powers that the Congo is our colony."

"All but one," said Roosevelt.

"America acknowledges our right to the Congo."

"America has a history of opposing imperialism wherever we find it," replied Roosevelt. "We threw the British out of our own country, and we're fully prepared to throw the Belgians out of the Congo."

"Just as, when you were President, you threw the Panamanians out of Panama?" asked Silva sardonically.

"America has no imperial claim to Panama. The Panamanians have their own government and we recognize it." Roosevelt paused. "However, we're not talking about Panama, but about the Congo."

Silva stared at Roosevelt. "For whom do you speak, Mr. Roosevelt?" asked Silva. "You are no longer President, so surely you do not speak for America."

"I speak for the citizens of the Congo."

Silva laughed contemptuously. "They are a bunch of savages who have no interest whatsoever in who rules them."

"Would you care to put that to a vote?" asked Roosevelt with a smile.

"So they vote now?"

"Not yet," answered Roosevelt. "But they will as soon as they are free to do so."

"And who will set them free?"

"*We* will," interjected Boyes from his seat halfway down the table.

"*You* will?" repeated Silva, turning to face Boyes. "I've heard about you, John Boyes. You have been in trouble with every government from South Africa to Abyssinia."

"I don't get along well with colonial governments," replied Boyes.

"You don't get along well with native governments, either," said Silva. He turned to Roosevelt. "Did you know that your companion talked the ignorant natives who proclaimed him their king into selling him Mount Kenya for the enormous price of four goats?"

"Six," Boyes corrected him with a smile. "I wouldn't want it said that I was cheap."

"This is ridiculous!" said Silva in exasperation. "I cannot believe I am hearing this! Do you really propose to conquer the Belgian Congo with a force of 53 men?"

"Absolutely not," said Roosevelt pleasantly.

"Well, then?"

"First," said Roosevelt, "it is the Congo, not the Belgian Congo. Second, we don't propose to conquer it, but to liberate it. And third, your intelligence is wrong. There are only 48 men in my party."

"48, 53—what is the difference?"

"Oh, there is a difference, Mr. Silva," said Roosevelt. He paused. "The other five are halfway to Nairobi by now."

"What do they propose to do once they get there?" asked Silva suspiciously.

"They propose to tell the American press that Teddy Roosevelt—who is, in all immodesty, the most popular and influential American of the past half century—is under military attack by the Belgian government. His brave little force is standing firm, but he can't hold out much longer without help, and if he should die while trying to free the citizens of the Congo from the yoke of Belgian tyranny, he wants America to know that he died at the hands of King Albert, who, I believe, has more than enough problems in Europe without adding this to his burden."

"You are mad!" exclaimed Silva. "Do you really think anyone will care what happens here?"

"That is probably just what the Mahdi said to Chinese Gordon at the fall of Khartoum," said Roosevelt easily. "Read your history books and you'll see what happened when the British people learned of his death."

"You are bluffing!"

"You are welcome to think so," replied Roosevelt calmly. "But in two months' time, 50,000 Americans will be standing in line to fight at my side in the Congo—and if you kill me, you can multiply that number by one hundred, and most of them will want to take the battle right to Belgium."

"This is the most preposterous thing I have ever heard!" exclaimed Silva.

Roosevelt reached into a pocket of his hunting jacket and pulled out a thick, official-looking document he had written the previous day.

"It's all here in black and white, Mr. Silva. I suggest that you deliver it to your superior as quickly as possible, because he'll want to send it on to Belgium, and I know how long these things take." He paused. "We'd like you out of the Congo in six months, so you can see that there's no time to waste."

"We are going nowhere!"

Roosevelt sighed deeply. "I'm afraid you are up against an historic inevitability," he said. "You have 20 armed men. I have 47, not counting myself. It would be suicidal for you to attack us here and now, and by the time you return from Stanleyville, I'll have a force of more than 30,000 Mangbetu plus a number of other tribes, who will not be denied their independence any longer."

"My men are a trained military force," said Silva. "Yours are a ragtag band of outcasts and poachers."

"But good shots," said Roosevelt with a confident grin. He paused again and the grin vanished. "Besides, if you succeed in killing me, you'll be the man who precipitated a war with the United States. Are you quite certain you want that responsibility?"

Silva was silent for a moment. Finally he spoke.

"I will return to Stanleyville," he announced. "But I will be back. This I promise you."

"We won't be here," answered Roosevelt.

"Where will you be?"

"I have no idea—but I have every intention of remaining alive until news of what's happening here gets back to America." Roosevelt paused and smiled. "The Congo is a large country, Mr. Silva. I plan to make many more friends here while awaiting Belgium's decision."

Silva got abruptly to his feet. "With this paper," he said, holding up the document, "you have signed not only your own death warrant, but the death warrant of every man who follows you."

Boyes laughed from his position halfway down the table. "Do you know how many death warrants have been issued on me? I'll just add this one to my collection." He paused, amused. "I've never had one written in French before."

"You are both mad!" snapped Silva, stalking off toward his men.

Roosevelt watched the assistant governor mount his horse and gallop off, followed by his twenty soldiers.

"I suppose we should have invited him to stay for dinner," he remarked pleasantly.

"You don't really think this is going to work, do you?" asked Boyes.

"Certainly."

"It's a lot of fancy talk, but it boils down to the fact that we're still only 53 men," said Boyes. "You'll never get the natives to go to war with the Belgians. They haven't any guns, and even if they did, we can't prepare them to fight a modern war in just six months' time."

"John, you know Africa and you know hunting," answered Roosevelt seriously, "but I know politics and I know history. The Congo is an embarrassment to the Belgians; Leopold wasted so much money here that his own government took it away from him two years ago. Furthermore, Europe is heading hell-for-leather for a war such as it has never seen before. The last thing they need is a battle with America over a piece of territory they didn't really want to begin with."

"They must want it or they wouldn't be here," said Boyes stubbornly.

Roosevelt shook his head. "They just didn't want anyone else to have it. When Africa was divided among the great powers in 1885, Belgium would have lost face if it hadn't insisted on its right to colonize the Congo, but it's been an expensive investment that has been a financial drain and a political embarrassment for more than two decades." He paused. "And what I said about General Gordon was true. He refused to leave Khartoum, and his death eventually forced the British government to take over the Sudan when the public demanded that they avenge him." Suddenly Roosevelt grinned. "A lot more people voted for me than ever even heard of Gordon. Believe me, John, the Belgian government will bluster and threaten for a month or two, and then they'll start negotiating."

"Well, it all sounds logical," said Boyes. "But I still can't believe that a force of 53 men can take over an entire country. It's just not possible."

"Once and for all, John, we are *not* a force of 53 men," said Roosevelt. "We are a *potential* force of a million outraged Americans."

"So you keep saying. But still—"

"John, I trust you implicitly when we're stalking an elephant or a lion. Try to have an equal degree of trust in me when we're doing what *I* do best."

"I wish I could," said Boyes. "But it just *can't* be this easy."

On December 3, 1910, five months and 27 days after receiving Roosevelt's demands, the Belgian government officially relinquished all claims to the Congo, and began withdrawing their nationals.

## VIII.

"*Damn* that Taft!"

Roosevelt crumpled the telegram, which had been delivered by runner from Stanleyville, in his massive hand and threw it to the ground. The sound of his angry, high-pitched voice combined with the violence of his gesture frightened a number of birds which had been searching for insects on the sprawling lawn, and they flew, squawking and screeching, to sanctuary in a cluster of nearby trees.

"Bad news, Mr. President?" asked Boyes.

They were staying at the house of M. Beauregard de Vincennes, a French plantation owner, some fifteen miles west of Stanleyville, on the shores of the Congo River. Three dozen of Roosevelt's men were camped out on the grounds, while the remainder were alternately hunting ivory and preparing the Lulua and Baluba, two of the major tribes in the area, for visits from Roosevelt himself.

"The man has no gratitude, no gratitude at all!" snapped Roosevelt. "I gave him the Presidency, handed it to him as a gift, and now I've offered to give him a foothold in Africa as well, and he has the unmitigated gall to tell me that he can't afford to send me the men and the money I've requested!"

"Is he sending anything at all?" asked Boyes.

"I requested ten thousand men, and he's sending six hundred!" said Roosevelt furiously. "I told him I needed at least twenty million dollars to build roads and extend the railroad from Uganda, and he's offering three million. Three million dollars for a country a third the size of the United States! *Damn* the man! J. P. Morgan may be a scoundrel and a brigand, but *he* would recognize an opportunity like this and pounce on it, I'll guarantee you that!" He paused and suddenly nodded his head vigorously. "By God, that's what I'll do! I'll wire Morgan this afternoon!"

"I thought he was your mortal enemy," remarked Boyes. "At least, that's the way it sounds whenever you mention him."

"Nonsense!" said Roosevelt. "We were on different sides of the political fence, but he's a competent man, which is more than I can say for the idiot sitting in the White House." Roosevelt grinned. "And he loves railroads. Yes, I'll wire him this afternoon."

"Are we refusing President Taft's offer, then?"

"Certainly not. We need all the manpower and money we can get. I'll wire our acceptance, and send off some telegrams to a few sympathetic newspaper publishers telling them what short shrift we're getting from Washington. I can't put any more pressure on Taft from here, but perhaps *they* can." Roosevelt shook his head sadly. "It serves me right for putting a fool in the White House. I tell you, John, if I didn't have a job to do right here, I'd go back to the States and take the nomination away from him in 1912. The man doesn't deserve to run a second time."

Roosevelt ranted against the "fat fool" in the White House for another fifteen minutes, then retired to his room to draft his telegrams. When he emerged an hour later for lunch, he was once again his usual pleasant, vigorous, optimistic self. Boyes, Bill Buckley, Mickey Norton, Yank Rogers, and Deaf Banks were sitting at a table beneath an ancient tree, and all of them except Banks, who hadn't heard the ex-President's approach, stood up as he joined them.

"Please be seated, gentlemen," said Roosevelt, pulling up a chair. "What's on the menu for this afternoon?"

"Salad and cold guinea hen in some kind of sauce," answered Norton. "Or that's what Madame Vincennes told me, anyway."

"I love guinea fowl," enthused Roosevelt. "That will be just bully!" He paused. "Good people, Monsieur and Madame Vincennes. I'm delighted that they offered to be our hosts." He paused. "This is much more pleasant than being cooped up in those airless little government buildings in Stanleyville."

"I hear we got some bad news from your pal Bill Taft," ventured Rogers.

"It's all taken care of," answered Roosevelt, confidently tapping the pocket that held his telegrams. "The men he's sending will arrive during the rainy season, anyway—and by the time the rains are over, we'll have more than enough manpower." He looked around the table. "It's time we considered some more immediate problems, gentlemen."

"What problems did you have in mind, sir?" asked Buckley, as six black servants approached the table, bearing trays of salad and drinks.

"We've had this country for two months now," answered Roosevelt. "It's time we began doing something with it—besides decimating its elephant population, that is," he added harshly.

"Well, we could decimate the Belgians that have stayed behind," said Buckley with an amused smile. "Billy Pickering would like that."

"I'm being serious, Mr. Buckley," said Roosevelt, taking a small crust of bread from his plate and tossing it to a nearby starling, which immediately picked it up and pranced off with it. "What's the purpose of making the Belgians leave if we don't improve the lot of the inhabitants? Everywhere we've gone we've promised to bring the benefits of democracy to the Congo. I think it's time we started delivering on that promise. The people deserve no less."

"Boy!" said Norton to one of the servants. "This coffee's cold. Go heat it up."

The servant nodded, bowed, put the coffee pot back on the tray, and walked toward the kitchen building.

"I don't know how you're going to civilize them when they can't remember from one day to the next that coffee's supposed to be served hot and not warm," said Norton. "And look at the way he's loafing: it could be hot when he gets it and cold by the time he brings it here."

"The natives don't drink coffee, so it can hardly be considered important to them," answered Roosevelt.

"They don't vote, or hold trial by jury, either," offered Buckley.

"Well, if we're to introduce them to the amenities of civilization, I think that voting and jury trials come well ahead of coffee drinking, Mr. Buckley."

"They can't even read," said Buckley. "How are you going to teach them to vote?"

"I plan to set up a public school system throughout the country," said Roosevelt. "The Belgian missionaries made a start, but they were undermanned and under-financed. In my pocket is a telegram that will appear in more than a thousand American newspapers, an open appeal to teachers and missionaries to come to the Congo and help educate the populace."

"That could take years, sir," noted Boyes.

"Ten at the most," answered Roosevelt confidently.

"How will you pay 'em, Teddy?" asked Rogers. "Hell, you can't even pay *us*."

"The missionaries will be paid by their churches, of course," said Roosevelt. "As for the teachers, I suppose we'll have to pay them with land initially."

"That might not sit too well with the people whose land we're giving away," noted Rogers.

"Yank, if there's one thing the Congo abounds in, besides insects and humidity, it's land."

"You say it'll take ten years to educate them," continued Rogers. "How will you hold elections in the meantime?"

"By voice," answered Roosevelt. "Every man and woman will enter the polling place and state his or her preference. As a matter of fact, there will probably be a lot less vote fraud that way."

"Did I hear you say that women are going to vote too, Teddy?" asked Yank Rogers.

"They're citizens of the Congo, aren't they?"

"But they don't even vote back home!"

"That's going to change," said Roosevelt firmly. "Our founding fathers were wrong not to give women the right to vote, and there's no reason to make the same mistake here. They're human beings, the same as us, and they deserve the same rights and privileges." Suddenly he grinned. "I pity the man who has to tell my Alice that she can't cast her vote at the polls. There won't be enough of him left to bury!"

"You know, we could raise money with a hut tax," suggested Buckley. "That's what the British have done wherever they've had an African colony."

"A hut tax?" asked Roosevelt.

Buckley nodded. "Tax every native ten or twenty shillings a year for each hut he erects. It not only raises money for the treasury, but it forces them to be something more than subsistence farmers, since they need money to pay the tax."

Roosevelt shook his head adamantly. "We're supposed to be freeing them, Mr. Buckley, not enslaving them."

"Besides," added Boyes, "it never worked that well in British East. If they didn't pay their hut tax, the government threw them into jail." He turned to Roosevelt and smiled. "You know what the Kikuyu and Wakamba called the jail in Nairobi? The King Georgi Hoteli. It was the only place they knew of where they could get three square meals a day and a free roof over their heads." He chuckled at the memory. "Once word of it got out, they were lining up to get thrown in jail."

"Well, there will be no such attempt to exploit the natives of the Congo," said Roosevelt. "We must always remember that this is *their* country and that our duty is to teach them the ways of democracy."

"That may be easier said than done," said Rogers.

"Why should you think so, Yank?" asked Roosevelt.

"Democracy's a pretty alien concept to them," answered Rogers. "It's going to take some getting used to."

"It was an alien concept to young Booker T. Washington and George Washington Carver, too," said Roosevelt, "but they seem to have adapted to it readily enough. It's never difficult to get used to freedom."

"We ain't talking freedom, Teddy," said Rogers. "They were free for thousands of years before the Belgians showed up, but they ain't never had a democracy. Their tribes are ruled by chiefs and witch doctors, not congressmen."

"And now that the Belgians are clearing out," added Norton, "our biggest problem is going to be to stop them from killing each other long enough to get to the polls."

"All of you keep predicting the most dire consequences," said Roosevelt irritably, "and yet you ignore the enormous strides the American Negro has taken since the Emancipation Proclamation. I tell you, gentlemen, that freedom has no color and democracy is not the special province of one race."

Boyes smiled, and Buckley turned to him.

"What are you looking so amused about, John? You've been here long enough to know everything we've said is the truth."

"You all think you're discouraging Mr. Roosevelt, and that if you tell him enough stories about how savage the natives are, maybe you'll convince him to join you long enough to kill every last elephant in the Congo and then go back to Nairobi." Boyes paused. "But I know him a little better than you do, and if there's one thing he can't resist, it's a challenge." He turned to Roosevelt. "Am I right, sir?"

Roosevelt grinned back at him. "Absolutely, Mr. Boyes." He looked around at his companions. "Gentlemen," he announced, "I've heard enough doomsaying for one day. It's time to roll up our sleeves and get to work."

## IX.

Roosevelt stared at his image in the full-length ornate gilt mirror that adorned the parlor of the state house at Stanleyville, and adjusted the tie of his morning suit.

"Good thing that little German tailor decided not to leave," he remarked to Boyes, who was similarly clad, "or we'd be conducting matters of state in our safari clothes."

"I'd be a damned sight more comfortable in them," replied Boyes, checking his appearance in the mirror, and deciding that his hair needed more combing.

"Nonsense, John," said Roosevelt. "We've got reporters and photographers from all over the world here."

"Personally, I'd much rather face a charging elephant," said Boyes, looking out the window. "I don't like crowds."

Roosevelt smiled. "I'd forgotten just how much I *miss* them." He put on his top hat and walked to the door. "Well, we might as well begin."

Boyes, unhappy and uncomfortable, and feeling quite naked without his pistol and rifle, followed the American out the front door to the raised wooden platform that had been constructed in front of the state house the previous day. The press was there, as Roosevelt had said: reporters and photographers from America, Belgium, England, France, Italy, Portugal, Kenya, and even a pair of Orientals had made the long, arduous trek to Stanleyville to hear this speech and record the moment for posterity. Seated on the front row of chairs, in a section reserved for VIPs and dignitaries, were the paramount chiefs of the Mangbetu, the Simba, the Mongo, the Luba, the Bwaka, the Zande, and the Kongo (which centuries ago had given the country its name). There was even a pair of pygmy chiefs, one of whom was completely naked except for a loincloth, a pair of earrings, and a necklace made of leopards' claws, while the other wore a suit that could have been tailored on Saville Row.

The crowd, some six hundred strong, and divided almost equally between whites and black Africans, immediately ceased its chattering when Roosevelt mounted the platform and waited in polite expectation while he walked to a podium and pulled some notes out of his pocket.

"Good morning, ladies and gentlemen. I thank you for your attendance and patience. I realize that, with our transportation system not yet constructed, you may have had some slight difficulty in reaching Stanleyville"—he paused for the good-natured laughter that he knew would follow—"but you're here now, and we're delighted to have you as the guests of our new nation."

He paused, pulled a brand-new handkerchief out of his pocket, and wiped away the sweat that had begun pouring down his face.

"We are here to proclaim the sovereignty of this beautiful land. Some years ago it was known as the Congo Free State. At the time, that was a misnomer, for it was anything but free. Today it is no longer a misnomer, and so it shall once again be known as the Congo Free State, an independent nation dedicated to the preservation of human dignity and the celebration of human endeavor."

A pair of blue turacos began shrieking in a nearby tree, and he smiled and waited a few seconds until the noise had subsided.

"What's past is past," he continued, "and the Congo Free State begins life with a clean slate. It bears no rancor toward any person or any nation that may have exploited its resources and its people in the past. But"—and here Roosevelt's chin jutted out pugnaciously—"this land will never be plundered or exploited again." He stared darkly out at his audience. "Never again will a privileged minority impose its will upon the majority. Never again will one tribe bear arms against another. Never again will women do most of the work and reap none of the benefits. And never again will the dreadful spectres of ignorance, poverty and disease run rampant in what Henry Stanley termed Darkest Africa." He raised his voice dramatically. "From this day forward, we shall illuminate the Congo Free State with the light of democracy, and turn it into the exemplar of Brightest Africa!"

Roosevelt paused long enough for his words to be translated, then smiled and nodded as the row of chiefs rose to their feet and cheered wildly, followed, somewhat less enthusiastically, by the Europeans.

"Thank you, my friends," he continued when the chiefs finally sat down. "We who have been fortunate enough to help in the birth of the Congo Free State have great plans for its future." He smiled triumphantly. "Great plans, indeed!" he repeated emphatically.

"Within two years, we will extend the East African Railway from its present terminus in Uganda all the way to Stanleyville, and within another year to Leopoldville. This will give us access to the Indian Ocean, as the Congo River gives us access to the Atlantic, and with the modern farming methods we plan to introduce, we will shortly be shipping exports in great quantity to both coasts."

There was more applause, a little less rabid this time, as most of the chiefs had only the haziest understanding of an economy that extended beyond their own tribes.

"We will construct public schools throughout the country," Roosevelt added. "Our goal is nothing less than 100% literacy by the year 1930."

This time the applause came only from the chiefs, as the whites in the audience looked openly skeptical.

"We will soon begin the construction of modern hospitals in every major city in the Congo Free State," continued Roosevelt, "and no citizen shall ever again want for medical care. American engineers will build dams the length of the Congo River, so that we can generate all the electricity that a modern nation will need. While leaving vast tracts of land untouched as national parks and game reserves, we will nonetheless crisscross the country with a network of roads, so that no village, no matter how remote, remains inaccessible."

He paused and glared at the disbelieving white faces in his audience.

"We will do everything I have said," he concluded. "And we will do it sooner than you think!"

The assembled chiefs began cheering and jumping around in their enthusiasm, and the remainder of the audience, sensing that he had concluded the major part of his address, applauded politely.

"And now, ladies and gentlemen, if you will all rise, we will, for the very first time, raise the flag of the Congo Free State." He turned to Boyes. "Mr. Boyes?"

Boyes withdrew the folded flag that he had been carrying inside his morning coat, waited for an honor guard of khaki-clad native soldiers to approach, and solemnly handed the flag over to their leader. The soldiers then marched to a recently-erected flagpole near the platform, and began raising a banner that depicted the colorful shields of twenty of the major tribes arranged in a pattern on a field of green, while Yank Rogers, who had been unable to create a national anthem on two days notice, played a military march on his ancient bugle. Roosevelt stood at attention and saluted, Boyes and the chiefs followed suit, and the reporters, politicians, and dignitaries were quick to rise to their feet as well.

When the flag had been raised and the rope secured at the base of the flagpole, Roosevelt faced the crowd once more.

"I have been selected, by the unanimous consent of the tribes that are represented here today, to draft and implement a democratic constitution for the Congo Free State. During this time I shall hold the office of Chief Administrator, an office that will be abolished when the first national election is held one year from today. At that time all the people of the Congo Free State, regardless of race or gender, will choose their own President and legislature, and their destiny will finally be in their own hands."

He stared out at the audience.

"I thank you for your attendance at this historic ceremony. Lunch will be provided for everyone on the lawn, and I will be available for interviews throughout the afternoon."

He climbed down from the platform to one last round of applause, finally allowed them a look at the famed Roosevelt grin, waited for Boyes to join him, and disappeared into the interior of the state house.

"How was I, John?" he asked anxiously.

"I thought you were excellent, Mr. President," answered Boyes truthfully.

"Mr. Chief Administrator, you mean," Roosevelt corrected him. Suddenly he smiled. "Although by this time you certainly know me well enough to call me Teddy. Everyone else does."

"I think I prefer Mr. President," replied Boyes. "I'm used to it."

Roosevelt shrugged, then looked out the window as the crowd began lining up at the long buffet tables.

"They don't think I can do it, do they, John?"

"No, sir, they don't," answered Boyes honestly.

"Well, they'd be correct if I applied their outmoded methods," said Roosevelt. He drew himself up to his full height. "However, this is a new century. We have new technologies, new methods, and new outlooks."

"But this is an old country," said Boyes.

"What is that supposed to mean, John?"

"Just that it might not be ready for your new approach, Mr. President."

"You saw the chiefs out there, John," said Roosevelt. "They're my strongest supporters."

"It's in their best interest to be," said Boyes. "After all, you've promised them the moon."

"And I'll deliver it," said Roosevelt resolutely.

## X.

Boyes walked into the state house and was ushered into Roosevelt's office.

"Where have you been, John?" asked Roosevelt. "I expected you back three days ago."

"It took a little longer than I thought to set up my trading company," answered Boyes. "But if your laborers ever arrive, at least they won't starve to death. I've got commitments for flour and meat."

"What are you trading for them?"

"Iodine," answered Boyes. "That's what took me so long. My shipment was late arriving from Nairobi."

"Iodine?" repeated Roosevelt, curious.

Boyes smiled. "There are some infections even a witch doctor can't cure." He sat down in a leather chair opposite Roosevelt's desk, looking quite pleased with himself. "An ounce of iodine for thirty pounds of flour or one hundred pounds of meat."

"That's immoral, John. Those people *need* that medication."

"Our people will need that food," answered Boyes.

"My hospitals will put you out of business," said Roosevelt sternly. "We will never withhold treatment despite a patient's inability to pay for it."

"When you build your hospitals, I'll find something else to trade them," said Boyes with a shrug. He decided to change the subject. "I hear you held your first local election while I was gone. How did it go?"

"I would call it a limited success."

"Oh?"

"It was a trial run, so to speak," said Roosevelt. "We selected a district at random and tried to show them how an election works." He paused. "We had a turnout of almost ninety percent, which is certainly very promising."

"Let me guess about the unpromising part," said Boyes. "Your candidates didn't get a single crossover vote."

Roosevelt nodded his head grimly. "The vote went one hundred percent along tribal lines."

"I hope you're not surprised."

"No, but I *am* disappointed." Roosevelt sighed. "I'll simply have to keep explaining to them that they are supposed to vote on the issues and not the tribal connections until they finally understand the principle involved."

For the first time since they had met, Boyes felt sorry for the American.

\* \* \*

"Not guilty?" repeated Roosevelt. "How in the name of pluperfect hell could they come in with a verdict of not guilty?"

He had turned the local theater into a courtroom, and had spent the better part of a week instructing the members of the Luba and Zande tribe in the intricacies of the jury system. Then he himself had acted as the presiding judge at the Congo Free State's very first trial by jury, and he was now in his makeshift chambers, barely able to control his fury.

"It was a unanimous decision," said Charlie Ross, who had acted as bailiff.

"I know it was a unanimous decision, Mr. Ross!" thundered Roosevelt. "What I don't know is how, in the face of all the evidence, they could come up with it?"

"Why don't you ask them?" suggested Ross.

"By God, that's exactly what I'll do!" said Roosevelt. "Bring them in here, one at a time."

Ross left the room for about five minutes, during which time Roosevelt tried unsuccessfully to compose himself.

"Sir," said Ross, re-entering in the company of a tall, slender black man, "this is Tambika, one of the jurors."

"Thank you, Mr. Ross," said Roosevelt. He turned to the African. "Mr. Tambika," he said in heavily-accented Swahili, "I wonder if you could explain your decision to me."

"Explain it, King Teddy?" asked Tambika, bewildered.

"Please call me Mr. Chief Administrator," said Roosevelt uncomfortably. He paused. "The man, Toma, was accused of stealing six cows. Four eyewitnesses claimed to see him driving the cows back toward his own home, and Mr. Kalimi showed you a bill of sale he received when he purchased the cows from Toma. There is no question that the cows bore the mark, or brand, of the plaintiff, Mr. Salamaki. Can you please tell me why you found him innocent?"

"Ah, now I understand," said Tambika with a large smile. "Toma owes me money. How can he pay me if he is in jail?"

"But he broke the law."

"True," agreed Tambika.

"Then you must find him guilty."

"But if I had found him guilty, he would never be able to pay me what he owes me," protested Tambika. "That is not justice, King Teddy."

Roosevelt argued with Tambika for another few minutes, then dismissed him and had Ross bring in the next juror, an old man named Begoni. After reciting the evidence again, he put the question to the old man.

"It is very clear," answered Begoni. "Toma is a Luba, as am I. Salamaki is a Zande. It is impossible for the Luba to commit a crime against the Zande."

"But that is precisely what he did, Mr. Begoni," said Roosevelt.

The old man shook his head. "The Zande have been stealing our cattle and our women since God created the world. It is our right to steal them back."

"The law says otherwise," Roosevelt pointed out.

"Whose law?" asked the old man, staring at him with no show of fear or awe. "Yours or God's?"

"If Mr. Toma were a Zande, would you have found him guilty?"

"Certainly," answered Begoni, as if the question were too ridiculous to consider.

"If Mr. Toma were a Zande and you knew for a fact that he had *not* stolen the cattle, would you have found him innocent?" asked Roosevelt.

"No."

"Why?" asked Roosevelt in exasperation.

"There are too many Zande in the world."

"That will be all, Mr. Begoni."

"Thank you, Mr. Teddy," said the old man, walking to the door. He paused for a moment just before leaving. "I like jury trials," he announced. "It saves much bloodshed."

"I can't believe it!" said Roosevelt, getting to his feet and stalking back and forth across the room after the door had closed behind Begoni. "I spent an entire week with these people, explaining how the system works!"

"Are you ready for the next one, sir?" asked Ross.

"No!" snapped Roosevelt. "I already know what he'll say. Toma's a tribal brother. Toma can't pay the bride price for his daughter if we throw him in jail. If a document, such as a bill of sale, implicates a Luba, then it must have been cursed by a Zande witch doctor and cannot be believed." Roosevelt stopped and turned to Ross. "What is the matter with these people, Charlie? Don't they understand what I'm trying to do for them?"

"They have their own system of justice, Mr. President," answered Ross gently.

"I've seen that system in action," said Roosevelt contemptuously. "A witch doctor touches a hot iron to the accused's tongue. If he cries out, he's guilty; if he doesn't, he's innocent. What kind of system is that, I ask you?"

"One they believe in," said Ross.

\* \* \*

"Well, that's that," said Roosevelt grimly, after opening the weekly mail. "Morgan isn't interested in investing in a railroad."

"Is there anyone else you can ask?" inquired Boyes.

"Bill Taft is mismanaging the economy. I have a feeling that the people who can afford to invest are feeling exceptionally conservative this year."

Nevertheless, he wrote another thirty letters that afternoon, each soliciting funds, and mailed them the next morning. He expressed great confidence that the money would soon be forthcoming, but he began making contingency plans for the day, not far off, when construction of the Trans-Congo Railway would be forced to come to a halt.

\* \* \*

"What do you mean, you have no more supplies?" demanded Roosevelt. "You had ample track for another five miles, Mr. Brody."

Brody, a burly American, stood uncomfortably before Roosevelt's desk, fidgeting with his pith helmet, which he held awkwardly in his huge hands.

"Yes, we did, Mr. Roosevelt."

"Well?"

"It's the natives, sir," said Brody. "They keep stealing it."

"Rubbish! What possible use could they have for steel track?"

"You wouldn't believe the uses they put it to, sir," answered Brody. "They use it to support their huts, and to make pens for their goats and cattle, and they melt it down for spearheads."

"Well, then, take it back."

"We were expressly instructed not to harm any of the natives, sir, and whenever we've tried to retrieve our tracks we've been threatened with spears, and occasionally even guns. If we can't take them back by force, they're going to stay right where they are until they rust."

"Who's the headman in your area, Mr. Brody?" asked Roosevelt.

"A Mangbetu named Matapoli."

"I know him personally," said Roosevelt, his expression brightening. "Bring him here and perhaps we can get this situation resolved."

"That could take six weeks, sir—and that's assuming he'll come with me."

Roosevelt shook his head. "That won't do, Mr. Brody. I can't pay your men to sit on their hands for six weeks." He paused, then nodded to himself, his decision made. "I'll return with you. It's time I got out among the people again, anyway."

He summoned Yank Rogers while Brody was getting lunch at a small restaurant down the street.

"What can I do for you, Teddy?" asked the American.

"I'm going to have to go to Mangbetu country, Yank," answered Roosevelt. "I want you and Mr. Buckley to remain in Stanleyville and keep an eye on things here while I'm gone."

"What about Boyes?" asked Rogers. "Isn't that his job?"

"John will be accompanying me," answered Roosevelt. "The Mangbetu seem to be very fond of him."

"They're equally fond of you, Teddy."

"I enjoy his company," said Roosevelt. He smiled wryly. "I'll also find it comforting to know that the state house hasn't been sold to the highest bidder in my absence."

\* \* \*

"John," remarked Roosevelt, as he and Boyes sat beside a campfire, "have you noticed that we haven't seen any elephant sign in more than a week now?"

The horses started whinnying as the wind brought the scent of lion and hyena to them.

"Perhaps they've migrated to the west," said Boyes.

"Come on, John," said Roosevelt. "I'm not as old a hand at this as you are, but I know when an area's been shot out."

"We've shipped a lot of ivory to Mombasa and Zanzibar during the past year," said Boyes.

"I didn't mind our men making a little money on the side, John, but I won't have them decimating the herds."

"They've been more than a year without a paycheck," answered Boyes seriously. "If you tell them they have to stop hunting ivory, I doubt that more than a dozen of them will stay in the Congo."

"Then we'll have to make do without their services," said Roosevelt. "The elephants belong to the people of the Congo Free State now. We've got to start a game department and charge for hunting licenses while there's still something left to hunt."

"If you say so," replied Boyes.

Roosevelt stared long and hard at him. "Will *you* be one of the ones who leaves, John?"

Boyes shook his head. "I'm the one who talked you into this in the first place, Mr. President," he answered. "I'll stay as long as you do." He paused thoughtfully. "I've made more than my share of money off the ivory anyway, and I suppose we really ought to stop while there are still some elephants left. I was just pointing out the consequences of abolishing poaching."

"Then start passing the word as soon as we get back," said Roosevelt. Suddenly he frowned. "That's funny."

"What is, sir?"

"I felt very dizzy for just a moment there." He shrugged. "I'm sure it will pass."

But it didn't, and that night the ex-President came down with malaria. Boyes tended to him and nursed him back to health, but another week had been wasted, and Roosevelt had the distinct feeling that he didn't have too many of them left to put the country on the right track.

\* \* \*

"Ah, my friend Johnny—and King Teddy!" Matapoli greeted them with a huge smile of welcome. "You honor my village with your presence."

"Your village has changed since the last time we were here," noted Boyes wryly.

Matapoli pointed proudly to the five railroad coach cars that his men had dragged miles through the bush over a period of months, and which now housed his immediate family and the families of four of the tribe's elders.

"Oh, yes," he said happily. "King Teddy promised us democracy, and he kept his promise." He pointed to one of the cars. "*My* democracy is the finest of all! Come join me inside it."

Roosevelt and Boyes exchanged ironic glances and followed Matapoli into the coach car, which was filled with some twenty or so of his children.

"King Teddy has returned!" enthused the Mangbetu chief. "We must have a hunt in the forest and have a feast in your honor."

"That's very thoughtful of you, Matapoli," said Roosevelt. "But it has been many months since we last saw each other. Let us talk together first."

"Yes, that would be very good," agreed Matapoli, puffing out his chest as the children recognized the two visitors and raced off to inform the rest of the village.

"Just how many children do you have?" asked Roosevelt.

Matapoli paused in thought for a moment. "Ten, and ten more, and then seven," he answered.

"And how many wives?"

"Five."

The puritanical American tried without success to hide his disapproval. "That's a very large family, Matapoli."

"Should be more, should be more," admitted the Mangbetu. "But it took many months to bring the democracies here."

"Had you left them on the track, you could have traveled all across the country on them," Boyes pointed out.

Matapoli threw back his head and laughed. "Why should I want to go to Lulua or Bwaka country?" he asked. "They would just kill me and take my democracies for themselves."

"Please try to understand, Matapoli," said Roosevelt. "There are no longer Mangbetu or Lulua or Bwaka countries. There is just the Congo Free State, and you all live in it."

"You are king of all the countries, King Teddy," answered Matapoli. "You need have no fear. If the Bwaka say that you are not, then we shall kill them."

Roosevelt spent the next ten minutes trying to explain the Congo Free State to Matapoli, who was no closer to comprehending it at the end of the discussion than at the beginning.

"All right," said the American with a sigh of resignation. "Let's get back to talking about the trains."

"Trains?" repeated Matapoli.

"The democracies, and the steel logs they rolled upon," interjected Boyes.

"Another gift from King Teddy," said Matapoli enthusiastically. "No longer can the leopards and the hyenas break through the thorns and kill my cattle. Now I use the metal thorns, and my animals are safe."

"The metal thorns were built so that you and the other Mangbetu could travel many miles without having to walk," said Roosevelt.

"Why should we wish to go many miles?" asked Matapoli, honestly puzzled. "The river runs beside the village, and the forest and its game are just a short walk away."

"You might wish to visit another tribe."

Matapoli smiled. "How could we sneak up on our enemies in the democracies? They are too large, and they would make too much noise when they rolled upon the iron thorns." He shook his head. "No, King Teddy, they are much better right here, where we can put them to use."

Long after the feast was over and Roosevelt and Boyes were riding their horses back toward Stanleyville, Roosevelt, who had been replaying the frustrating day over and over in his mind, finally sighed and muttered: "By God, that probably *is* the best use they could have been put to!"

Boyes found the remark highly amusing, and burst into laughter. A moment later Roosevelt joined him with a hearty laugh of his own, and that was the official end of the Trans-Congo Railway.

* * *

They came to a newly-paved road when they were fifteen miles out of Stanleyville and, glad to finally be free of the bush and the forest, they veered their mounts onto it. As they continued their journey, they passed dozens of men and women walking alongside the road.

"Why don't they walk *on* it, John?" asked Roosevelt curiously. "There can't be fifteen trucks in the whole of the Congo. Until we import some more, we might as well put the roads to some use."

"They're barefoot," Boyes pointed out.

"So what? The road is a lot smoother than the rocks alongside it."

"It's also a lot hotter," answered Boyes. "By high noon you could fry an egg on it."

"You mean we've spent a million dollars on roads for which there not only aren't any cars and trucks, but that the people can't even walk on?"

"This isn't America, sir."

"A point that is being driven home daily," muttered Roosevelt wearily.

## XI.

Roosevelt sat at his desk, staring at a number of letters and documents that lay stacked neatly in front of him. To his left was a photograph of Edith and his children, to his right a picture of himself delivering a State of the Union address to the United States Congress, and behind him, on an ornate brass stand, was the flag of the Congo Free State.

Finally, with a sigh, he opened the final letter, read it quickly, and, frowning, placed it atop the stack.

"Bad news, Mr. President?" asked Boyes, who was sitting in the leather chair on the opposite side of the desk.

"No worse than the rest of them," answered Roosevelt. "That was from Mr. Bennigan, our chief engineer on the Stanley Falls Bridge. He sends his regrets, but his men haven't been paid in three weeks, and he's going to have to pull out." He stared at the letter. "There's no postmark, of course, but I would guess that it took at least two weeks to get here."

"We didn't need him anyway," said Boyes, dismissing the matter with a shrug. "What's the sense of building a bridge over the falls if we don't have any trains or cars?"

"Because someday we'll have them, John, and when we do, they're going to need roads and tracks and bridges."

"When that happy day arrives, I'm sure we'll have enough money to complete work on the bridge," replied Boyes.

Roosevelt sighed. "It's not as devastating a blow as losing the teachers. How many of them have left?"

"Just about all."

"Damn!" muttered Roosevelt. "How can we educate the populace if there's no one to teach them?"

"With all due respect, sir, they don't need Western educations," said Boyes. "You're trying to turn them into Americans, and they're not. Reading and writing are no more important to them than railroads are."

Roosevelt stared at him for a long moment. "What do *you* think is important to them, John?"

"You're talking about a primitive society," answered Boyes. "They need to learn crop rotation and hygiene and basic medicine far more than they need roads that they'll never use and railroad cars that they think are simply huts on wheels."

"You're wrong, John," said Roosevelt adamantly. "A little black African baby is no different than a little black American baby—or a little white American baby, for that matter. If we can get them young enough, and educate them thoroughly enough . . ."

"I don't like to contradict you, sir," interrupted Boyes, "but you're wrong. What's the point of having ten thousand college graduates if they all have to go home to their huts every night because there aren't two hundred jobs for educated men in the whole country? If you want to have a revolution on your hands, raise their expectations, prepare them to live and function in London or New York—and then make them stay in the Congo."

Roosevelt shook his head vigorously. "If we did things your way, these people would stay in ignorance and poverty forever. I told you when we began this enterprise that I wasn't coming here to turn the Congo into my private hunting preserve." He paused. "I haven't found the key yet, but if anyone can bring the Congo into the 20th Century, I can."

"Has it occurred to you that perhaps no one can?" suggested Boyes gently.

"Not for a moment," responded Roosevelt firmly.

"I'll stay as long as you do, sir," said Boyes. "You know that. But if you don't come up with some answers pretty soon, we may be the last two white men in this country, except for the missionaries and some of the Belgian planters who stayed behind. Almost half our original party has already left."

"They were just here for ivory or adventure," said Roosevelt dismissively. "We need people who care about this country more than we need people who are here merely to plunder it." Suddenly he stared out the window at some fixed point in space.

"Are you all right, sir?" asked Boyes after Roosevelt had remained motionless for almost a minute.

"Never better," answered the American suddenly. "You know, John, I see now that I've been going about this the wrong way. No one cares as much for the future of the Congo as the people themselves. I was wrong to try to bring in help from outside; in the long run, any progress we make here will be much more meaningful if it's accomplished by our own efforts."

"Ours?" repeated Boyes, puzzled. "You mean yours and mine?"

"I mean the citizens of the Congo Free State," answered Roosevelt. "I've been telling you and the engineers and the teachers and the missionaries what they need. I think it's about time I told the people and rallied them to their own cause."

"We've already promised them democracy," said Boyes. "And there's at least one Mangbetu village that will swear we delivered it to them," he added with a smile.

"Those were politicians' promises, designed to get our foot in the door," said Roosevelt. "Democracy may be a right, but it isn't a gift. It requires effort and sacrifice. They've got to understand that."

"First they've got to understand what democracy means."

"They will, once I've explained it to them," answered Roosevelt.

"You mean in person?" asked Boyes.

"That's right," said Roosevelt. "I'll start in the eastern section of the country, now that my Swahili has become fluent, and as I move west I'll use translators. But I'm going to go out among the people myself. I'm certainly not doing any good sitting here in Stanleyville; it's time to go out on the stump and get my message across to the only people who really need to understand it." He paused. "I'd love to have your company, John, but there are so few of us left that I think it would be better for you to remain here and keep an eye on things."

"Whatever you say, Mr. President," replied Boyes. "When will you leave?"

"Tomorrow," said Roosevelt. He paused. "No. This afternoon. There's nothing more important to do, and we've no time to waste."

* * *

He went among the people for five weeks, and everywhere he stopped, the drums had anticipated his arrival and the tribes flocked to see him.

He took his time, avoided any hint of jingoism, and carefully explained the principles of democracy to them. He pointed out the necessity of education, the importance of modern farming methods, the need to end all forms of tribalism, and the advantages of a monied economy. At the end of each "town meeting," as he called them, he held a prolonged question-and-answer session, and then he moved on to the next major village and repeated the entire procedure again.

During the morning of his thirty-sixth day on the stump, he was joined by Yank Rogers, who rode down from Stanleyville to see him.

"Hello, Yank!" cried Roosevelt enthusiastically as he saw the American riding up to his tent, which had been pitched just outside of a Lulua village.

"Hi, Teddy," said Rogers, pulling up his horse and dismounting. "You're looking good. Getting out in the bush seems to agree with you."

"I feel as fit as a bull moose," replied Roosevelt with a smile. "How's John doing?"

"Getting rich, as usual," said Rogers, not without a hint of admiration for the enterprising Yorkshireman. "I thought he was going to be stuck with about a million pounds of flour when all the construction people pulled out, but he heard that there was a famine in Portugese Angola, so he traded the flour for ivory, and then had Buckley and the Brittlebanks brothers cart it to Mombasa when they decided to call it quits, in exchange for half the profits."

"That sounds like John, all right," agreed Roosevelt. "I'm sorry to hear that we've lost Buckley and the others, though."

Rogers shrugged. "They're just Brits. What the hell do they know about democracy? They'd slit your throat in two seconds flat if someone told them that it would get 'em an audience with the King." He paused. "All except Boyes, anyway. He'd find some way to put the King on display and charge money for it."

Roosevelt chuckled heartily. "You know, I do believe you're right."

"So much for Mr. Boyes," said Rogers, "How's your campaign going?"

"Just bully," answered Roosevelt. "The response has been wildly enthusiastic." He paused. "I'm surprised news of it hasn't reached you."

"How could it?" asked Rogers. "There aren't any radios or newspapers—and even if there were, these people speak 300 different languages and none of 'em can read or write."

"Still," said Roosevelt, "I've made a start."

"I don't doubt it, sir."

"I'm drawing almost five hundred natives a day," continued Roosevelt. "That's more than 15,000 converts in just over a month."

"If they stay converted."

"They will."

"Just another six million to go," said Rogers with a chuckle.

"I'm sure they're passing the word."

"To their fellow tribesmen, maybe," answered Rogers. "I wouldn't bet on their talking to anyone else."

"You sound like a pessimist, Yank," said Roosevelt.

"Pessimism and realism are next-door neighbors on this continent, Teddy," said Rogers.

"And yet you stay," noted Roosevelt.

Rogers smiled. "I figure if anyone can whip this country into shape, it's you—and if you do, I want to be able to laugh at all those Brits who gave up and left."

"Well, stick around," said Roosevelt. "I'm just getting warmed up."

"Sounds like fun," said Rogers. "I haven't heard you rile up a crowd since you ran for Governor of New York. I was in Africa before you ran for President." Suddenly he reached into his shirt pocket and withdrew an envelope. "I almost forgot why I rode all this way," he said, handing it to Roosevelt.

"What is it?"

"A letter from Boyes," answered Rogers. "He said to deliver it to you personally."

Roosevelt opened the letter, read it twice, then crumpled it into a ball and stuffed it into a pocket.

"I'm afraid you're not going to be able to hear me giving any speeches this week, Yank," he announced. "I've got to return to Stanleyville."

"Something wrong?"

Roosevelt nodded. "It seems that Billy Pickering found four Belgian soldiers in a remote area in the southwest, men who had never received word that the Belgians had withdrawn from the Congo, and shot them dead."

"You mean he had me ride all the way here just for that?" demanded Rogers.

"It's a matter of vital importance, Yank."

"What's so important about four dead men?" asked Rogers. "Life is cheap in Africa."

"The Belgian government is demanding reparation."

"Yeah, I see where *that* can make it a little more expensive," admitted Rogers.

## XII.

"I wasn't sure how you wanted to handle it," Boyes said, staring across the desk at Roosevelt, who had just returned to Stanleyville less than an hour ago.

"You were right to summon me, John."

"So far they haven't made any threats, but we're receiving diplomatic communiqués every other day."

"What's the gist of them?"

"Reparation, as I mentioned in my note to you."

Roosevelt shook his head. "They know we don't have any money," he answered. "They want something else."

"Pickering's head on a platter, I should think," suggested Boyes.

"They don't care any more about their soldiers than *he* did," said Roosevelt. "Let me see those communiqués."

Boyes handed over a sheaf of papers, and Roosevelt spent the next few minutes reading through them.

"Well?" asked Boyes when the American had set the papers down.

"I don't have sufficient information," answered Roosevelt. "Have they gone to the world press with this?"

"If they have, we won't know it for months," said Boyes. "The most recent paper I've seen is a ten-week-old copy of the *East African Standard*." He paused. "Why would going to the press make a difference?"

"Because if they've gone public, then they're positioning themselves to try to take the Congo back from us, by proving that we can't protect European nationals."

"But they weren't nationals," said Boyes. "They were soldiers."

"That just makes our position worse," replied Roosevelt. "If we can't protect a group of armed men who know the Congo, how can we protect anyone else?"

"Then what do you want to do about Pickering?" inquired Boyes.

"Where is he now?"

"In the jail at Leopoldville. Charlie Ross brought him in dead drunk, and locked him away."

"The proper decision," said Roosevelt, nodding approvingly. "I must remember to commend him for it."

"I'm afraid you won't be able to, Mr. President," said Boyes. "He's back in Kenya."

"Charlie?" said Roosevelt, surprised. "I'd have thought he'd be just about the last one to leave."

Boyes paused and stared uncomfortably across the desk at Roosevelt.

"Except for Yank Rogers and me, he was."

"They're *all* gone?"

"Yes, sir." Boyes cleared his throat and continued: "You did your best, sir, but everything's coming unraveled. Most of them stuck it out for better than two years, but we always knew that sooner or later they'd leave. They're not bureaucrats and administrators, they're hunters and adventurers."

"I know, John," said Roosevelt, suddenly feeling his years. "And I don't hold it against them. They helped us more than we had any right to expect." He paused and sighed deeply. "I had rather hoped we'd have a bureaucracy in place by this time."

"I know, sir."

"I wonder if it would have done much good," Roosevelt mused aloud. He looked across at Boyes. "That trip I just returned from—I wasted my time, didn't I?"

"Yes, sir, you did."

"We needed more teachers," said Roosevelt. "One man can't educate them overnight. We needed more teachers, and more money, and more time."

Boyes shook his head. "You needed a different country, Mr. President."

"Let's have no more talk about the inferiority of the African race, John," said Roosevelt. "I'm not up to it today."

"I've never said they were inferior, Mr. President," said Boyes, surprised.

"Certainly you have, John—and frequently, too."

"That's not so, sir," insisted Boyes. "No matter what you may think, I have no contempt or hatred for the Africans—which is why I've always been able to function in their countries." He paused. "I understand them—as much as any white man can. They're not inferior, but they *are* different. The things that are important to us are of no consequence to them, and the things they care about seem almost meaningless to us—and because of that, you simply can't turn them into Americans in two short years, or even twenty."

"We did it in America," said Roosevelt stubbornly.

"That's because your blacks were being assimilated into a dominant society that already existed and was in possession of the country," answered Boyes. "The whites here are just passing through, and the Africans know it, even if the whites don't. They may have to put up with us temporarily, but we won't have any lasting effect on their culture." He paused as Roosevelt considered his words, then continued: "When all is said and done, it's their country and their continent, and one of these days they're going to throw us all out. But what follows us won't look anything like a Western society; it'll be an African society, shaped by and for the Africans." He smiled wryly. "I wish them well, but personally I wouldn't care to be part of it."

"I've said it before, John: You're a very interesting man," said Roosevelt, a strange expression on his face. "Please continue."

"Continue?" repeated Boyes, puzzled.

"Tell me why you wouldn't care to be part of an African nation based on African principles and beliefs."

"For the same reason that they have no desire to become Americans or Europeans, once we stop bribing them to pretend otherwise," answered Boyes. "Their culture is alien to my beliefs." He paused. "Democracy, and the Christian virtues, and the joys of literature, and a reverence for life, all these things work for you, sir, because you have a deep and abiding belief in them. They won't work here because the people of the Congo *don't* believe in them. They believe in witch doctors, and tribalism, and polygamy, and rituals that seem barbaric to me even after a quarter century of being exposed to them. We couldn't adapt to their beliefs any more than they can adapt to ours."

"Go on, John," said Roosevelt, his enthusiasm mounting.

Boyes stared at him curiously. "You've got that look about you, Mr. President."

"What look?"

"The same one I saw that first night we met in the Lado Enclave," said Boyes.

"How would you describe it?" asked Roosevelt, amused.

"I'd call it the look of a crusader."

Roosevelt chuckled with delight. "You're a very perceptive man, John," he said. "By God, I wish I were a drinking man! I'd celebrate with a drink right now!"

"I'll be happy to have two drinks, one for each of us, if you'll tell me what you're so excited about, Mr. President," said Boyes.

"I finally understand what I've been doing wrong," said Roosevelt.

"And what is that, sir?" asked Boyes cautiously.

"*Everything!*" said Roosevelt with a hearty laugh. "Lord knows I've had enough discussions on the subject with you and the others, but I've always proceeded on the assumption that I was part of the solution. Well, I'm not." He paused, delighted with his sudden insight. "I'm part of the problem! So are you, John. So are the British and the French and the Portuguese and the Belgians and everyone else who has tried to impose their culture on this continent. That's what you and Mickey Norton and Charlie Ross and all the others have been telling me, but none of you could properly articulate your position or carry it through to its logical conclusion." He paused again, barely able to sit still. "*Now* I finally see what we have to do, John!"

"Are you suggesting we leave?" asked Boyes.

Roosevelt shook his head. "It's not that simple, John. Eventually we'll have to, but if we leave now, the Belgians will just move back in and nothing will have changed. It's our duty—our holy mission, if you will—to make sure that doesn't happen, and that the Congo is allowed to develop free from all external influences, including ours."

"That's a mighty tall order, sir," said Boyes. "For instance, what will you do about the missionaries?"

"If they've made converts, they're here at the will of the people, and they've become part of the process," answered Roosevelt after some consideration. "If they haven't, eventually they'll give up and go home."

"All right," said Boyes. "Then what about—?"

"All in good time, John," interrupted Roosevelt. "We'll have to work out thousands of details, but I feel in my bones that after two years of false starts, we're finally on the proper course." He paused thoughtfully. "Our first problem is what to do with Billy Pickering."

"If you're worried about the Belgians, we can't give him a trial by jury," said Boyes. "These people have hated the Belgians for decades. They'll find him innocent of anything more serious than eliminating vermin, and probably vote him into the Presidency."

"No, we can't have a jury trial," agreed Roosevelt. "But not for the reason you suggest."

"Oh?"

"We can't have it because it's a Western institution, and that's what we're going to eradicate—unless and until it evolves naturally."

"Then do you want to execute him?" asked Boyes. "That might satisfy the Belgians."

Roosevelt shook his head vigorously. "We're not in the business of satisfying the Belgians, John." He paused thoughtfully. "Have Yank Rogers escort him to the nearest border and tell him never to return to the Congo. If the Belgians want him, let *them* get him."

Having summarily eliminated the system of justice that he had imposed on the country, Roosevelt spent the remainder of the week eagerly dismantling the rest of the democracy that he had brought to the Congo.

# XIII.

Roosevelt was sitting beneath the shade of an ancient baobab tree, composing his weekly letter to Edith. It had been almost three weeks since he had embraced his new vision for the future of the Congo, and he was discussing it enthusiastically, in between queries about Kermit, Quentin, Alice, and the other children.

Boyes sat some distance away, engrossed in Frederick Selous' latest memoirs, which had been personally inscribed to Roosevelt, whose safari he had arranged some three years earlier.

Suddenly Yank Rogers walked up the broad lawn of the state house and approached Roosevelt.

"What is it, Yank?"

"Company," he said with a contemptuous expression on his face.

"Oh?"

"Our old pal, Silva," said Rogers. "You want me to bring him to your office?"

Roosevelt shook his head. "It's too beautiful a day to go inside, Yank. I'll talk to him right here."

Rogers shrugged, walked around to the front of the building, and returned a moment later with Gerard Silva.

"Hello, Mr. Silva," said Roosevelt, getting to his feet and extending his hand.

"*Ambassador* Silva," replied Silva, shaking his hand briefly.

"I wasn't aware that Belgium had sent an Ambassador to the Congo Free State."

"My official title is Ambassador-at-Large," said Silva.

"Well, you seem to have come a long way since you were an Assistant Governor of an unprofitable colony," said Roosevelt easily.

"And *you* have come an equally long way since you promised to turn the Congo into a second America," answered Silva coldly. "All of it downhill."

"It's all a matter of perspective," said Roosevelt.

There was an uneasy silence.

"I have come to Stanleyville for two reasons, Mr. Roosevelt," said Silva at last.

"I was certain that you wouldn't come all this way without a reason," replied Roosevelt.

"First, I have come to inquire about the man, Pickering."

"Mr. Pickering was deported as an undesirable some 19 days ago," answered Roosevelt promptly.

"Deported?" demanded Silva. "He killed four Belgian soldiers!"

"That was hearsay evidence, Mr. Silva," responded Roosevelt. "We could find no eyewitnesses to confirm it."

"Pickering himself admitted it!"

"That was why he was deported," said Roosevelt. "Though there was insufficient evidence to convict him, we felt that there was every possibility that he was telling the truth. This made him an undesirable alien, and he was escorted to the border and told never to return."

"You let him go!"

"We deported him."

"This is totally unacceptable."

"We are a free and independent nation, Mr. Silva," said Roosevelt, a hint of anger in his high-pitched voice. "Are you presuming to tell us how to run our internal affairs?"

"I am telling you that this action is totally unacceptable to the government of Belgium," said Silva harshly.

"Then should Mr. Pickering ever confess to committing a murder within the borders of Belgium, I am sure that your government will deal with it in a manner that it more acceptable to you." Roosevelt paused, as Boyes tried not to laugh aloud. "You had a second reason for coming to Stanleyville, I believe?"

Silva nodded. "Yes, I have, Mr. Roosevelt. I bring an offer from my government."

"The same government that is furious with me for deporting Mr. Pickering?" said Roosevelt. "Well, by all means, let me hear it."

"Your experiment has been a dismal failure, Mr. Roosevelt," said Silva, taking an inordinate amount of pleasure in each word he uttered. "Your treasury is bankrupt, your railroads and highways will never be completed, your bridges and canals do not exist. You have failed to hold the national election that was promised to the international community. Even the small handful of men who accompanied you at the onset of this disastrous misadventure have deserted you." Silva paused and smiled. "You must admit that you are in an unenviable position, Mr. Roosevelt."

"Get to the point, Mr. Silva."

"The government of Belgium is willing to put our differences behind us."

"How considerate of them," remarked Roosevelt dryly.

"If you will publicly request our assistance," continued Silva, "we would be willing to once again assume the responsibility of governing the Congo." He smiled again. "You really have no choice, Mr. Roosevelt. With every day that passes, the Congo retreats further and further into insolvency and barbarism."

Roosevelt laughed harshly. "Your government has a truly remarkable sense of humor, Mr. Silva."

"Are you rejecting our offer?"

"Of course I am," said Roosevelt. "And you're lucky I don't pick you up by the scruff of the neck and throw you clear back to Brussels."

"Need I point out that should my government decide that the Congo's vital interests require our presence, you have no standing army that can prevent our doing what must be done?"

Roosevelt glanced at his wristwatch. "Mr. Silva," he said, "I'm going to give you exactly sixty seconds to say good-bye and take your leave of us. If you're still here at that time, I'm going to have Mr. Boyes escort you to the nearest form of transportation available and point you toward Belgium."

"That is your final word?" demanded Silva, his face flushing beneath his deep tan.

"My final word is for King Albert," said Roosevelt heatedly. "But since I am a Christian and a gentleman, I can't utter it. Now get out of my sight."

Silva glared at him, then turned on his heel and left.

Roosevelt turned to Boyes, who was still sitting in his chair, book in hand. "You heard?" he asked.

"Every word of it." Boyes paused and smiled. "I wish he'd have stayed another forty seconds." He got to his feet and approached Roosevelt. "What do you plan to do about the Belgians?"

"We certainly can't allow them back into the country, that much is clear," said Roosevelt.

"How do you propose to stop them?"

Roosevelt lowered his head in thought for a moment, then looked up. "There's only one way, John."

"Raise an army?"

Roosevelt smiled and shook his head. "What would we pay them with?" He paused. "Besides, we don't want a war. We just want to make sure that the Congo is allowed to develop in its own way, free from all outside influences."

"What do you plan to do?" asked Boyes.

"I'm going to return to America and run for the Presidency again," announced Roosevelt. "Bill Taft is a fat fool, and I made a mistake by turning the country over to him. I'll run on a platform of making the Congo a United States Protectorate. *That* ought to make the Belgians think twice before trying to march in here again!" He nodded his head vigorously. "That's what I'll have to do, if these people are ever to develop their own culture in their own way." His eyes reflected his eagerness. "In fact, I'll leave this afternoon! I'll take Yank with me; I'm sure I can find a place for him in Washington."

"You realize what will happen if you lose?" said Boyes. "The Belgians will march in here five minutes later."

"Then there's no time to waste, is there?" said Roosevelt. "You're welcome to come along, John."

Boyes shook his head. "Thank you for the offer, Mr. President, but there's still a few shillings to be made here in Africa." He paused. "I'll stay in Stanleyville until you return, or until I hear that you've lost the election."

"A little more optimism, John," said Roosevelt with a grin. "The word 'lose' is not in our lexicon."

Boyes stared at him for a long moment. "You mean it, don't you?" he said at last, as the fact of it finally hit home. "You're really going to run for the Presidency again."

"Of course I mean it."

"Don't you ever get tired of challenges?" asked Boyes.

"Do you ever get tired of breathing?" replied Roosevelt, his face aglow as he considered the future and began enumerating the obstacles he faced. "First the election, then Protectorate status for the Congo, and then we'll see just what direction its social evolution takes." He paused. "This is a wonderful experiment we're embarking upon, John."

"It'll be interesting," commented Boyes.

"More than that," said Roosevelt enthusiastically. "It'll be bully—just bully!"

\* \* \*

The date was April 17, 1912.

# XIV.

*After returning home from the Congo, Theodore Roosevelt was denied the Republican nomination for President in 1912. Undaunted, he formed the Bull Moose party, ran as its presidential candidate, and was believed to be ahead in the polls when he was shot in the chest by a fanatic named John Chrank on October 14. Although he recovered from the wound, he was physically unable to campaign further and lost the election to Woodrow Wilson, though finishing well ahead of the seated Republican President, William Howard Taft. He lost what remained of his health in 1914 while exploring and mapping the River of Doubt (later renamed the Rio Teodoro) at the behest of the Brazilian government, and never returned to Africa. He died at his home in Sagamore Hill, New York, on January 6, 1919.*

*John Boyes made and lost three more fortunes in British East Africa, spent his final days driving a horse-drawn milk wagon in Nairobi, and died in 1951.*

*The Belgian Congo (later renamed Zaire) was granted its independence in 1960, and held the first and only free election in its history. This was followed by three years of the most savage inter-tribal bloodletting in the history of the continent.*